A Faithful Boy's Influence

by
Aunt Friendly

author of "Timid Lucy",
"Fidgetty Skeert" and others

~and the story of~

Ears For Little Gleaners

by
Herbert Dawson

D1545534

Grace & Truth Books
Sand Springs, Oklahoma

ISBN # 1-58339-106-1
Originally published in 1862 by William Martien Publishing,
Pittsburg, PA
Published by Triangle Press, 1995
Previously published under the title "All Can Help"
Current edition, by Grace & Truth Books, 2004

Cover design by Ben Gundersen

Grace & Truth Books
3406 Summit Boulevard
Sand Springs, Oklahoma   74063
Phone: 918 245 1500

www.graceandtruthbooks.com
email: info@graceandtruthbooks.com

TABLE OF CONTENTS

*Charlie turned towards Meedville with
the great basket on his arm.*

Chapter 1

An Icy Morning

Ice! Ice! Everywhere! Ice on the ground, ice on the ground, ice on the trees, ice on the fences – the very houses coated with ice! So it was at Meedville one Sunday morning in December, yet the church-bell rang out as cheerily as if it were the merry month of May, and the gate to the churchyard was thrown as wide open as if the broad walk were not one sheet of treacherous ice, promising a downfall to any who dared to venture on it. A heavy mist was in the air, and there was a continual rattling sound, as the trees dropped morsels of their frozen coating, when their branches waved in the wind.

Would anybody venture out on such a day? The sexton seemed to think so, for he pulled the bell-rope as if he was sure that he was accomplishing a good end.

At Meedville there were some church-goers who never stayed at home for wind or weather, and Mrs. Berridge and her family were among them. The good lady herself, and her two daughters, would as soon have thought of putting out their own eyes, as neglecting the sound of that well-known bell. In their seats they were sure to be when the minister entered the chancel; that is, their bodies were sure to be there, wherever else their minds might chance to be wandering.

On this particular morning they had a stranger with them; not one of the tall, dignified men, nor one of those fashionably dressed ladies, who occasionally appeared there, but a boy in his grey roundabout coat – a boy, evidently not more than fourteen years of age.

The stranger was enough of a gentleman to walk up the middle aisle in advance of the party and throw wide open the door of the third pew for Mrs. Berridge and her daughters to pass in. This feat Miss Augusta Berridge accomplished without any injury to her garments in squeezing through the narrow passage. Little Annie followed, imitating her sister's movements with great care, and perching herself at length on the seat, with a satisfied air as if the business of the morning was over, and now she had nothing to do but look about her and see who was at church.

Annie had moved her head from side to side and pointed with her nose at all the people down one aisle, and had actually counted twenty, when she noticed that her cousin Charlie was still on his knees. What could he be about all this time?

It did not once cross Annie's mind that Charles Clement was entering, for the first time, a church where he expected to worship for a whole year, and that he might feel this an occasion for special prayer. She could not know that he was asking that he might ever find his Heavenly Father near him in that humble sanctuary, and that he might be himself a faithful hearer of the messages which the appointed clergyman should bring to his soul.

Of course Annie Berridge could not know all this; she did not even guess it, for to serious thoughts she was herself a stranger. Moreover, she had not in the least suspected that her cousin Charlie was of what she called "a religious turn." She had not seen him, so far as she could remember, till the evening before, and then he had been so merry and agreeable that she fancied he must always be in a frolic.

Charlie Clement knew that there was "a time to laugh," and that this was not a suitable time, he plainly thought; for when Augusta Berridge turned her face towards him and gave it a comical, mocking twist as the minister entered the chapel, there was a very sober look in Charlie's eye, instead of the answering smirk which she expected.

The service went on. Charlie did not see Augusta passing her quick glances over the congregation; he did not notice the quiet munching of candy with which Annie contented herself; nor did he see that Mrs. Berridge's thoughts were far from the Holy Book on which her eyes were bent.

Mrs. Berridge had a respect for religion. She liked a devout manner in church. She wanted to set a good example; but she had not come up to the Lord's house to praise Him for all His mercies and to call upon Him for forgiveness, and for that Holy

Spirit He delights to bestow on all who ask. Her service was vain, fair as it was in outside show.

For once, on this day, there was a *true* worshipper in Mrs. Berridge's pew. Augusta looked at her cousin Charles in astonishment. He seemed really interested in what he was about, and when the sermon began, he listened as if he wanted to hear; he listened respectfully, like one who expected to be taught a lesson worth learning.

The young clergyman was by no means unattractive in appearance. There was a look of earnest thought about his face, but no traces of genial warmth, or any kind of consciousness of the outer world. During the prayers he was forgotten, for he spoke with quiet simplicity; but in the pulpit he seemed windy and wordy, rather than truly addressing the people on matters of significance to them. His sermons were fine essays on the beauty of Divine truth, but seemed intended to reach no particular persons and to produce no particular effect.

"O, how good it is to get out into the fresh air!" exclaimed Augusta Berridge, as she stepped from the church door. "Dreadfully dull! Was it not, Charlie?"

Charlie was fairly startled by the sudden loud tones of his companion. A silence, that she should have recognized as reproof, was his reply. He had been taught that there should be a reverence as one left the house of God, as from the presence of a king; no noise in the ante-chamber, no rude haste in laying aside the garment of solemnity suited to such an audience.

"O! Cousin Charlie! Hold me up! I certainly shall fall!" said Annie, putting her foot timidly on the ice-covered steps.

The lad helped the little girl tenderly down, and then joined Mrs. Berridge and Augusta, who were waiting for him below.

"Isn't he tiresome? Rev. Mayer, I mean," said Augusta, as they walked along.

"He cannot help it, my child. Poor young man! We must be patient with him. Nobody likes him, and I suppose he knows it. For my part, I am sorry for him, though it is quite a trial to have such dull preaching," said the mother.

Charles looked up in astonishment, but said simply, "Has Rev. Mayer been settled here long?"

"Only half a year. The bishop recommended him and the vestry took him without much thought. He ranked high at the seminary, but why, I cannot imagine," Mrs. Berridge replied.

"I should think he was a man of talents and might be very agreeable in conversation," said Charles.

"Nobody knows much about that; he visits very little. He seems shy – uncommonly shy! I never could bear a bashful man," said Mrs. Berridge.

"I mean to go and see him," remarked Charlie; "I like to know my minister."

Augusta turned her sharp blue eyes quickly upon Charlie to see if he was smiling, but he looked perfectly sober, and she began to laugh, replying,

"I think I see him going through the torture of your visit! First he rises, as if he had a cramp in the knees; then out goes his arm, as if it were jerked out with an invisible string. Before you have time to fairly shake his hand, down it drops, and he looks you straight in the eyes, as if to ask you, 'What's your business, young man?' Say, Charlie, may I go with you?"

"No, no! But cousin, I do really mean to go see him!" replied Charlie. So the conversation ended as the family reached Mrs. Berridge's pleasant home.

Chapter 2

A Boyish Visitor

Charles Clement was the oldest son in a family of six, and his mother was a widow. It was not strange that he felt himself quite a man, as for three years he had been his mother's companion, and frequently her adviser. The younger children looked up to him as a remarkable person and many of his schoolmates and friends were of the same opinion.

That Charlie was not at all unaware of his own powers was plain from his decided step and the particularly erect manner in which he carried himself. But there was nothing of pride or arrogance in his air; and in his round, cheerful face he held a bright, sunny expression which seemed to promise a willingness to always find a way to do a kindness to others.

Charlie would have packed up his trunk, if occasion had required it, and traveled from Maine to Georgia alone, with the composure of a man of forty years of age. He had so long done the honours in his own home, and kept a watchful, protective eye upon his mother, that there was a kind of manliness about him, rare to find in a lad of his age.

When Charlie dressed himself on Monday morning, with special care, before paying his visit to the reverend, he had no idea that he was about to do a thing from which nearly any other boy would shrink.

He had no difficulty in finding the humble lodging of Rev. Mayer; humble, for though the people of Meedville expect a minister unequalled in talent and piety, they had no intents of giving him a salary which would provide more than a bare subsistence.

Charlie knocked twice before any notice was taken of his arrival. It was plain that it was Monday in every sense of the word in that establishment, a true washing-day, when all things must give way to the weekly purification. A little woman with a bonnet on, and a wet dress pinned up round her waist, at length made her appearance from the rear of the house. She opened her eyes with astonishment, when instead of the supposed "fish-man," Master Charlie Clement stood before her, with his cap in hand.

"Is the Rev. Mayer at home?" said Charlie, with his usual composure.

"Yes. I don't know. Yes, I'll see," said the woman, in evident confusion; whether at her own lamentably moist condition, or at the unexpected appearance of a visitor at that time, on a Monday morning, it was hard to decide.

The woman of the bonnet disappeared at a side-door, without asking the stranger to walk in.

Master Charlie, however, made bold to take a few steps into the hall, and there he awaited her return.

He had stood there just long enough to note the thread-bare condition of the faded carpet, and the paintless arms of the wood chair, when, not the woman, but quite another person appeared. A tall young man, in a calico dressing-gown, came out from the aforementioned side-door and looked inquiringly at Charlie.

Charlie did not at first recognize in the person who stood before him, the Rev. Mr. Mayer of the preceding day. The young man was very pale and a mass of dark hair was standing in wild confusion, straight off from his forehead. His brown eyes stared absently, as if he had just been roused from sleep. The fact was, he had been deep in the composition of a sermon. His head been resting on his hands and his fingers thrust into his hair when he was called to see "some young chap at the door, asking for the minister."

"Is this the Rev. Mr. Mayer?" said Charlie, after a moment of doubtful silence.

"Yes, yes," said Rev. Mayer, struggling to keep his sermon out of mind and attend to the matter at hand.

"My name is Charles Clement," said the lad, stepping forward and putting out his hand.

A name unknown to fame, it seemed to be to Rev. Mayer. He did not see the offered hand, but said:

"Well, sir, what is it you wish this morning?"

"Perhaps I have come upon you at a busy time," said Charles, politely.

"I *was* writing, but" – and the minister looked inquiringly at the boy, "but I can attend to you now."

"I have no particular business, I can call at some other time," said Charlie, retiring.

Rev. Mayer gave a puzzled look at his visitor, and driving from his thoughts a "thirdly" point in his sermon, said pleasantly and welcomingly,

"Won't you walk in now?"

"I thank you, not this morning, sir," said Charlie, decidedly, "but I should like to come again, for I want to know my minister."

As he spoke, he again put out his hand and looked up frankly into Rev. Mayer's face.

Rev. Mayer took the offered hand and said, shyly, "Yes, come again, I shall be glad to see you."

With another bow and a pleasant "good morning" from Charles, the interview was over.

Charlie Clement was more amused than annoyed at the result of his proposed call on the pastor. He had made a beginning and he was not disheartened.

Chapter 3

A Step Nearer

Mrs. Berridge had thought it necessary to introduce her nephew at the academy, where he was to be a pupil. Charlie would by no means have hesitated to appear there alone, but he politely assented, when his aunt proposed to accompany him.

Some domestic duties had kept her at home on Monday morning, and Charlie, as we have seen, took the opportunity to put in a wedge towards an acquaintance with his minister.

If Rev. Mayer had been spoken of respectfully, the lad would have felt inclined to treat him with all due deference; indeed, Charlie had been taught that a certain peculiar politeness and reverence was due to those whose office it is to minister in spiritual things.

The light and unkind manner in which Rev. Mayer was spoken of had, however, called out a yet warmer feeling in Charlie Clement towards him than might otherwise have been his own. Yes, Charlie resolved, for his part, that he would treat his minister with respect and affection, and to be by no means influenced by what others might say about him.

As for how to go about the further pursuit of making his acquaintance, Charlie was somewhat puzzled. Though by no means of a bashful nature, he hesitated about risking another call, when it appeared that such visits were most unexpected, if not unwelcome. Time for calling anywhere, Charlie had little or none that week, after he had fairly entered upon his studies. Although he did not "burn the midnight oil," it was after nine o'clock before his books were laid aside, and he was ready to fall into such sound sleep as only happy, healthy youth can enjoy.

After this week of constant occupation, Saturday, with its holiday hours, was most welcome. Breakfast was hardly over when Charlie produced a pair of skates and declared his intention of having enough good exercise on the ice to take the chill out of him for a week to come!

The boys on the neighbouring pond soon found out that the new scholar was likely to rank number one among the skaters, as well as in his classes. Such cutting of letters and such skilful maneuvers as Charlie was able to perform had not often been seen on Meedville pond!

The academy bell at length called home the merry party to dinner. Tutor and pupils vanished like ice in a thaw. Charlie stopped to take a few more successful turns, after the coast was clear, and when there was no danger of knocking over small boys and unskillful skaters, who did not know how to keep out of other people's way.

However, after such an outing on the ice, dinner indeed sounded appealing to Charlie, and he too turned his face homeward. He had not gone far on his return when he saw an old woman stepping cautiously along the slippery path, some distance before him. She had a basket on her arm, which, though evidently not heavy, made it more difficult for her to keep her balance. The wooden cane that she carried was but a poor security against a downfall on the treacherous ice which everywhere covered the ground. At length, after executing some extraordinary dancing steps, she fell down hard, while basket and cane deserted her, and she lay helpless on the ground.

Charlie rushed to her side and was there in a moment; but in vain he attempted to raise her.

"O my! I am done for! Dear! Dear!" the lady exclaimed. "Now I never! What shall I do?"

"Do? Why just get on my team here," said a cheerful voice at her side.

The speaker, a rough-looking countryman, was driving a wood-sled; and with a loud "whoa" to his horses, he jumped down and began to suit his actions to the words. "Never fear, Katy Brown; you'll do well enough. You just got hoisted; that was all. Here now; come up!" And his strong arms placed her on the sled and leaned her against a meal-sack, which was now his only load.

"My, my! Jack – what's to become of my basket? What's the man to do without his clothes,

13

and Sunday coming! You could drive round to Meedville, I s'pose."

"How I wish I could, Katy," said the same hearty voice; "but you know I'm not my own master, and farmer Watkins don't let us idle our time."

"No more he don't, true enough!" said Katy, significantly. "I could lie by, tomorrow bein' Sunday; but what's to become of the clothes?"

"Where do they belong?" asked Charlie, giving a look at the great basket.

They're his'n, the preacher's, of course. I don't wash for nobody else," said the woman.

"Rev. Mayer, do you mean?" asked Charlie, brightening.

"Yes, child; asking questions don't help, though," said the old woman, fretfully.

"But I mean to do more," said Charlie, taking up the basket; "I'll take them home for you."

"And I'll see to the old woman; so here goes," and Jack Tyler raised his whip, as if to warn his horses to start.

"Stop, stop! Where do you live?" said Charlie, addressing the woman.

"That ain't no odds!" was the short answer.

"The first red house in among the pines, a piece along this road," said the man. "Shame, Katy, to speak so to the young gentleman!" And then, with a whisper not meant for Katy's ear, he added to Charlie, "She'll need some looking after, likely enough."

"I ain't too deaf to hear that," said the old woman, with a keen look; but it was plain that the words had escaped her.

Jack Tyler did not stay for any more conversation. He went his way; and Charlie turned towards Meedville, with the great basket on his arm.

Charlie Clement never troubled himself as to who laughed at him. All the boys in the village might have hooted at him for carrying a washerwoman's basket, and he would not have cared. He was not naturally sensitive to such taunts; and moreover, when he was sure he was doing a kind action, the opinion of the world was of little consequence to him. He stood up, therefore, on the door-step of Rev. Mayer's boarding-house, on the main street, not noticing the crowd of boys who were coming down the sidewalk, full of holiday fun. A shower of snowballs first apprized him of their approach; and cries of "How much do you ask a dozen? There goes the washer-boy!" sounded in his ears.

"Six shillings a dozen! Six shillings a dozen, my boys!" sang out Charlie, in a merry tone.

A face was seen for a moment at a lower window, and then the door was thrown open wide, and Rev. Mayer appeared.

The crowd of boys dispersed in a moment, and Charlie was about to give up his basket when Rev. Mayer said, quite heartily, "Come in, come in." He had not forgotten the bright, pleasant face that had looked so warmly at him the Monday before.

Charlie did step in; but it was only to explain how he became the bearer of the basket, and to say that he now had no time to spare, as his aunt's dinner hour had arrived.

"I am grieved to hear that Katy has taken a fall! I want to go and see her," said Rev. Mayer, thoughtfully. "Charlie, do you know where she lives?"

"I could find it, I think. I mean to go there this afternoon myself," said Charlie, promptly.

"Then we will go together, if you like it," said Rev. Mayer.

"I should like it right well," said Charlie.

"At three o'clock, then, you will call for me," said Rev. Mayer.

"At three o'clock, sir. Good-bye, sir," was Charlie's reply.

Chapter 4

Katy Brown

Three o'clock found Charlie Clement punctually at Rev. Mayer's door, and the minister was there to meet him.

"I have often wanted to go to see Katy, but she never seemed to like the idea," said the minister, as they walked along.

"We may not get the pleasantest welcome in the world," said Charlie, smiling, "but the farmer's man seemed to think she might need help, for all that."

Charlie had often been with his mother to the homes of the poor, and to him the visit seemed quite a common occurrence. With Rev. Mayer, the case was different. During his stay at boarding-school, he had prepared for four years at college; three more he had passed at a theological seminary. Motherless from his birth, he had never known the sweet joys of home or the innocent pleasures of society. No loving hand had led him to the haunts of poverty and taught him how to minister to the poor.

Yet God had chosen Marshall Mayer to be peculiarly His servant and the messenger of His truth and mercy. The studious senior, at college, had become an earnest Christian; and when the world offered him an occupation where his talents might have made for him a great name and a large income, he had instead chosen the service of Christ as his calling, and had given up every object in life, save that of serving his heavenly Master.

While Rev. Mayer had been pronounced dry in the pulpit, and shy and unsociable in private life, his heart was burning with desire to do good. He had not been silent in his closet, either. Earnestly and faithfully, he had prayed to be made a fit instrument for the heavenly work and to be guided in the path of usefulness. Such prayers are never unanswered. Marshall Mayer might seem for a time an unprofitable servant, yet he would not be driven out of the vineyard in shame and disgrace. He had to overcome the effects of a life of seclusion, and a natural sensitiveness that was his constant scourge, ere he could be a useful pastor. Would he succeed?

Rev. Mayer found it a real pleasure to be walking through the clear, cold air, with his cheerful companion at his side. With a lad like Charlie, his diffidence was not in his way, and conversation flowed naturally on. They had passed the village and were on the country road, when Charlie asked, "Is there to be a confirmation held here soon, sir?"

"The bishop is to visit us in February, but I do not know whether there will be any persons to be confirmed," said the minister, with a painful blush.

"I hope there will be one," said Charlie, and he took Rev. Mayer's hand as he spoke.

The boy's frank face was full of earnest feeling that was not to be mistaken.

"We must know each other better," said Rev. Mayer, with a hearty grasp of the hand that had been placed in his. "I hope that you may be that one, and be ready for the holy rite."

These few confidential words seemed to have placed Rev. Mayer and Charlie upon a different footing. The shy clergyman found himself talking freely to the boy at his side, of all his hopes and his wishes, his purposes and his prayers.

Charlie felt the force of the deep piety that welled up from his companion's heart, and his own resolution to devote himself to his Master's service was strengthened and redoubled.

Katy Brown's red house among the pines was easily found, and there, at the window, sat Katy herself, knitting away, as if nothing had happened.

"We will go in, now we are here," said Rev. Mayer, who having screwed up his courage to the visit, was not willing to give it up.

Their knock was answered by a cry of "Come in," but no one appeared at the door.

The visitors obeyed, and found themselves in the single room, which was Katy's dwelling-place, her home truly; for it had a roof over it, and a chimney to carry up the smoke from her pipe and her fire.

The pipe Katy now laid aside, and through her horn spectacles she looked up inquiringly at the visitors. The glance satisfied her as to who they were, and she hastened to say,

"Were not the clothes right, sir – eh?" and she gave a doubtful look at Charlie.

"All quite right, Katy," said Rev. Mayer, helping himself to a seat, Charlie following his example. "All quite right; but I was afraid you were not right yourself, after your fall. Are you lame yet?"

"No more than I always am," said Katy quickly. "Old folks don't expect to be spry."

"And yet you take this long, cold walk every week. I had no idea you lived so far from the village," said Rev. Mayer, kindly.

"How should you know? You never were here before," said Katy.

"I thought you did not care to have visitors," said the minister, truthfully.

"No more I didn't," said Katy, "but now you are come, put up your feet to the fire afore you start away."

Rev. Mayer accepted the strangely offered courtesy, and drew his chair nearer to the wide chimney-corner.

"Are you not lonely here sometimes, Katy?" he said.

"Like enough, I am. Buryin' children ain't a cheerful business, and I've done enough of it in my day. I shall be goin' too, soon," was the muttered reply.

"Going to a better country, I hope, Katy," said Rev. Mayer kindly.

"No such a thing! I ain't one of the good ones," said the old woman. "I never was, and I'm too old now. I needn't expect nothin' better than I deserve."

The free, full forgiveness that Christ offers to sinners was present now to the young minister's mind. On that he built his own hope, and he longed to bring it home to the poor old creature before him, but she would not give him time.

"It ain't no use!" she broke in upon him, as his lips parted. "It ain't no use. I've worried and fretted all along of the years that is gone. If I was young, I'd begin again. Take the right start, boy," she said, turning suddenly to Charlie. "Take a right start. Old folks can't learn new ways."

"I want to start right," said Charlie, earnestly.

The conversation was here interrupted by a loud double knock, followed by the immediate sound of Jack Tyler's heavy step on the floor.

Jack started back when he saw the visitors, but concluded, on the whole, to stay and do his errand. With a side bow to Rev. Mayer, before speaking, he turned to Katy and said, "It's like to be slippery as ever in the morning, Katy; I shall go to church in the old sleigh, and will take you along. Will you go? Eh, Katy?"

"Like enough! Like enough, Jack! But here, as you're ready to be a-toting, maybe you'll give these folks here a lift," and she looked thoughtfully at her visitors.

It seemed that Katy was tired of her company, yet she was half-pleased at their visit, too.

"If you can ride standin', sir, I'd be glad to have you on my sled," said Jack, with a bow to Rev. Mayer, that swept round far enough to include Charlie in the invitation.

"Thank you, thank you! We will not refuse such an offer," replied Rev. Mayer. Then, going up to Katy, he shook her withered hand and said, in a low, earnest voice, "Good-bye Katy; remember, it is never too late to begin a new life."

The old woman shook her head, but made no answer.

They saw her wrinkled face at the window, watching them as they mounted the sled, and Jack said, "She's glad to see you, even though she behaves so queer. The poor woman leads a lonesome life, and she likes to see somebody now and then, even if it's only to say a cross word to."

Jack stood up firmly on his sled, with the reins in one hand and the whip in the other, but Rev. Mayer and Charlie had to hold fast to the upright poles at the corners of the rude vehicle, to keep their footing. Bump, bump, they went over the rough masses of frozen snow, and for a time conversation was quite impossible. Rev. Mayer had food enough for thought. He was dwelling on the sight he had just witnessed – an aged human being, ready to sink into the grave, without hope, without one cheering ray to lighten the dark valley.

This painful subject so completely occupied his mind, that he at first did not even notice the conversation that arose between Charlie and the young countryman, as soon as they were on a smoother portion of the road.

Charlie was a lover of out-of-door sports, and was interested in all Jack could tell him of the fish in a trout-stream a mile or so away, or of the game that might be started in the very woods through which they were driving.

Then followed anecdotes of dogs, and Charlie grew quite animated in speaking of a former pet of his, who was so constantly with him that he had to be locked up on Sunday morning, to keep him from following his master to Sunday-school.

"Sunday-school!" said Jack thoughtfully. "I always wished I'd a went when I was a boy."

"We had a nice Bible-class at home where there was two or three fellows as old as you," said Charlie.

Rev. Mayer had heard nothing while the talk was of game and dogs, but now a subject was touched upon more in unison with his own thoughts, and he became conscious of what was going on around him.

"A Bible-class, did you say, Charlie?", and at the moment the thought struck the minister that such an undertaking might be a means of doing good in this very town.

"Yes, a Bible-class: our minister taught it; and how we all did enjoy it!"

Rev. Mayer was silent a moment. "I have no aptness in teaching. I never had a Sunday-school class. I am afraid it would be a failure," he thought. Still, conscience whispered, "You had better try. God can give strength for anything it is His will that we should do. Here seems to be an opening. Go forward!"

"We might have a Bible-class here," said Rev. Mayer, thoughtfully.

"O, I should like it so much," said Charlie, heartily; "and you would go, wouldn't you?" he added, turning to Jack.

"I'd be a poor scholar enough," said Jack, giving a doubtful look at the minister.

"No one is a poor scholar who really wants to learn," said Rev. Mayer. "We will meet at my study tomorrow evening, and try to make a beginning."

"I'll be there, never fear," said Jack, decidedly.

At this moment they reached a side road, which turned off just as the scattered houses betokened the entrance to Meedville.

"I go this way," said Jack, turning his horses' heads towards the corner, and bringing them to a full stop.

"Then we must get off, and thank you for helping us so far on our way," said Rev. Mayer, stepping out upon the crisp snow as he spoke.

Away drove Jack, whistling as he went, while Rev. Mayer and Charlie walked on, side by side, talking of the Bible-class, until they reached the minister's door.

A bonnet had been thrust out of that same door every five minutes for the last half-hour, and a face within it had looked eagerly up the street. The last look was a satisfied one, as it espied Rev. Mayer approaching, for the door was shut decidedly, as bonnet and wearer disappeared to the portion of the house where strangers were inadmissible.

"It is almost supper-time, I declare," said Rev. Mayer, looking wistfully at Charlie; "won't you stop and take a cup of tea with me?"

"Not to-night, but I thank you, sir. Aunt expects to have some company for me at home," said Charlie; and with an affectionate shake of the hand, he bade the minister good-bye.

Rev. Mayer's small study looked especially attractive to him that evening. Perhaps it was because his good landlady, Mrs. Toombs, had taken the opportunity to give it a cleaning during his absence; perhaps it was because he was cheered by the knowledge that, at last, one of his parishioners was turning towards him with affectionate confidence! Even the tea-table seemed to him to have a more attractive air than usual, though Mrs. Toombs maintained her customary silence. Going about her domestic duties, in her little brown hood and stout apron, she seemed quite another woman than when at the head of her table, in her clean, white cap and black alpacca dress; so entirely different a person, that she did not seem to dare open her lips, lest she should speak out of character. At any rate, something always kept her silent in the minister's presence. He might as well have taken his meals alone, for what little conversation her company imparted; but she was useful in her own way, and she knew it. She filled the minister's cup with tea before he perceived it was out, and kept his plate supplied with such fare as the table afforded, while he went on eating, lost in his own thoughts.

A slight rattling at the tea-try was the general indication that supper was over, and he obeyed this hint as regularly as he did the bell that announced the meal was ready.

Rev. Mayer was very, very happy in his study that evening. Sermon after sermon he glanced at – none would suit him for the morrow. It was late before he saw what was before him; he must write, he must prepare a message that would reach at least one heart among his people! And after earnest prayer to Him who was to send that message to him, Rev. Mayer took his pen in hand.

The clock ticked not for him; not for him was the noise of the passer-by. He was lost, absorbed in the declaration of the good news to mankind – a Savior dying for the world, an ascended Lord calling all the weary unto Him.

Chapter 5

Poor Fun

Augusta Berridge was in the parlour, standing before the mirror. It was plain that she considered herself in full dress, in the sense of uncommonly well-dressed, and was altogether satisfied on that account. Augusta was wearing, for the first time, a skirt that swept the floor as she walked, and she had promenaded the room two or three times, looking over her shoulder to see the half a quarter of a yard of blue silk trail along the carpet. Annie, meanwhile, was equally occupied in endeavoring to catch glimpses of the great bow which tied her new sash.

They both started and looked a little ashamed as Charlie came in on them, fresh from his long walk.

"Why, Charlie! You are not dressed!" said Augusta, in surprise.

"Am I late?" said Charlie, looking at his watch in a manly way, as if he had worn it always (he had had it only a week). "Half-past five! I did not think it was so late. Moonlight and twilight coming together misled me."

It did not take Charlie Clement long to clean up. With him, it was a simple matter of business to be clean; to be well-done, of course, but not to fuss over it with any needless degree of thought. He was in the parlour before the first clattering ring at the door announced that one of the guests had arrived.

The new-comer, Master Henry DeWitt, needed no one to introduce him. It was plain that he and Augusta were old acquaintances, and Charlie he had already seen at school.

Harry DeWitt was very tall for fourteen, and glad for his height, for he held up his head as straight as a militia colonel on parade.

"Where were you this afternoon, that you did not go skating?" said Harry, taking a comfortable chair and settling himself into it.

"I walked into the country with Rev. Mayer," replied Charlie frankly.

"With Rev. Mayer?" said Harry, holding up both hands. "Oh my! I don't envy you the task."

"That's the kind of business that suits Charlie," said Augusta, laughing. "He pretends to be very much pleased with Rev. Mayer."

"I do like him, heartily," said Charlie, with evident warmth. "I wish I could see more of him."

Harry gave a low whistle and Augusta shrugged her shoulders.

The boys and girls now came in by twos and threes, until all the guests had arrived. Thirteen bright young faces were gathered round the table, all full of life and merriment.

Harry DeWitt was about to say what he considered a capital remark, when Augusta gave him a sudden nudge and pointed significantly at Charlie.

Charlie was standing opposite to his aunt. Mrs. Berridge waved her hand, and there was a moment of silence.

In a few simple words, Charlie returned thanks for the blessings of food showered by the Lord's hand upon them, and then he took his seat as comfortably as if he had but just been speaking to some human companion at his side. Charlie had so long been accustomed to 'saying grace' at his mother's table that it seemed to him a sort of matter of course, a pleasant part of the meal, not to be omitted. Mrs. Berridge had been enough at Mrs. Clement's to be aware of this fact, and now, at her own table, she was glad to see carried out what she considered an excellent habit.

Charlie Clement had been but a single week at Meedville, yet he was beginning to have his influence there. The slightest thread casts a shadow, and even a young person is ever doing something for good or evil, by his example.

A bold, determined, upright spirit like Charlie's always has its admirers and its imitators. The best scholar and the best skater in the academy must wield a power strong for good or evil.

This short, simple prayer had been for Charlie a kind of public profession, telling plainly on which side he stood. Did he lose the respect of his companions by it? There were two or three who smiled during his praying, and one little girl (more silly than the rest) had trouble suppressing a senseless giggle; but the effect on most of the company was to make them feel that Charlie Clement was a person to be looked up to, a person who knew his duty and dared to do it.

Augusta Berridge had a great store of games at her command, and was herself most skillful in playing them all. There was no lack of fun among the young people, and Charlie Clement's cheerful, natural laugh was heard again and again.

At length a new game was proposed. One of the company was to go out, and return, impersonating some character, whom the rest were to guess, from the act.

Harry DeWitt went first, and paraded the room, calling out:

> *"With head erect, you fancy how*
> *Arms locked behind,*
> *As if to balance the prone brow,*
> *Oppressive with its mind."*

Quickly, several of them shouted at once, "Napoleon!"

Charlie Clement went next, and with a lantern in his hand went about the room, peering into every face, and was recognized as Diogenes seeking an honest man. Aristides, writing his own name on a shield, and Anne Boleyn offering her slender neck to the executioner, had all been impersonated and recognized by the group of players.

It was now Augusta Berridge's turn to go out. She soon returned, wearing an old cloth cloak, so long that it hid even the much-admired dress which trailed behind her. A tall beaver hat was on her head. She had but to walk across the room, in a slow, peculiar gait, when cries of "Rev. Mayer! Rev. Mayer!" were heard from all sides of the room. But with this she was not content, but began to say, in a voice designed to be a mock counterpart of Rev. Mayer's, "Dearly, beloved brethren – ", ever so slowly, and with a smirk.

"Now that is too bad, Augusta!" said Charlie, indignantly. "Rev. Mayer is our minister, and you owe him respect on that account, even if you do not like him."

Augusta threw down the cloak and hat, and exclaimed, "I don't see why I may not have a little fun at his expense, even if he is a minister."

"The king of a country revenges the disrespect offered to his herald; and a minister is the herald of the King of kings, and should be treated accordingly. I use my mother's words," said Charlie warmly. "I think you owe some respect to the office, Augusta, whatever you may think of the man!"

"What is all this?" said Mrs. Berridge, coming in at the moment.

"Only Charlie giving us a sermon," said Augusta, laughing.

"Go on, Charlie; I should like to be a hearer," said Mrs. Berridge, taking a seat on the sofa.

"No! No! Let us play elements!" said Annie, who was impatient to have this controversy over so the frolic might continue. But the sight of an approaching tray of delicious delights called off her attention, and pyramids of ice-cream were soon the focus of everyone's interest.

The company now broke up into little circles, and Charlie had an opportunity to carry out a plan which he had in mind all the evening.

"Augusta was too hard on Rev. Mayer," said Harry DeWitt. "You were correct to reprove her."

"Indeed she was," said Joseph White, the oldest boy in the company.

The conversation having turned upon the clergyman, Charlie took occasion now, after speaking affectionately of him, to mention the Bible-class, and actually obtained a promise from Harry and Joseph at least to try it for the first evening. Not that Harry or Joseph had the slightest desire to improve in the best of knowledge. Their Sunday evenings were simply dull at home; this would be an excuse for going out, and "might not, after all, be so bad," said they to one another on their way home.

The Bible-class! That was the chief thing in Charlie Clement's mind that night; not the frolic of the evening, not angry feelings towards Augusta; but the new Bible-class, a fresh opportunity to be improved, a new Sunday joy, a new step on the heavenly road.

Chapter 6

Good Seed

The Sunday morning service was over, and the people of Meedville were scattering away to their homes. Rev. Mayer had preached on the encouraging words of our Savior, "Whosoever cometh unto Me, I will in no wise cast out." Simply, tenderly, earnestly, this blessed promise had been urged upon the attention of the hearers. The elderly, burdened with many years of sin, and the child, just beginning to struggle with its evil heart, were called upon to accept the merciful invitation of Jesus and trust themselves to Him.

Annie Berridge had soon found out that cousin Charlie was fond of children, and was never better pleased than when he had her at his side or on his knee. That morning, he had passed a pleasant hour with her, telling her Bible stories, and when she left him, full of thanks for his kindness, he had won from her a promise to "be a good girl at church, and try to listen to the sermon."

Annie kept her promise that Lord's Day! And during that morning's sermon, Rev. Mayer's faithful words had, for the first time, stirred in Annie's heart a yearning to be one of the Saviour's little ones, a wish to know what it was to truly bow to the Lord Jesus as one's King. Her sister Augusta, by contrast, had not a thought of listening either to service or sermon. Though bodily present during the time of solemn worship, her mind was far away, dwelling on the plans and pleasures of the week to come.

A habit of inattention at church! A trifling sin, some would suppose to think it. Is it a small sin to insult the Most High in His own sanctuary? Is it a matter of no consequence to shut the ears to the voice of prayer and turn the thoughts from the words of exhortation that might win the heart to the highest of all things? Some of the grandest avenues of good and finest opportunities of improvement are robbed, when listless inattention becomes a habit in church.

Augusta was in her usual frivolous state when she left the church door, and out of the abundance of the heart did her mouth speak.

Annie paid but little attention while her sister remarked on the dress of their friends and acquaintances in the other pews; but when Augusta began to speak of Rev. Mayer, Annie's attention was gained, as she said:

"Oh! How I do wish Rev. Mayer would simply go away and somebody more interesting would come! My bones fairly ached before the sermon was over! I don't believe he knows what he is talking about himself."

Augusta would not have willingly given pain to her little sister's body, even by the scratch of a pin. Yet little did she know that she was now doing her sister's soul a fearful and horrid wrong. For little Annie looked up to Augusta as one far smarter and wiser than herself, and so now Annie felt ashamed that the sermon she had been so moved by were words that Augusta regarded as so tiresome. So Annie's half-formed resolutions to be a better girl were checked, the tender feeling in her heart passed away, and she was ready to add her idle words to the worthless ones that her sister was uttering.

Those gossiping tales at the church door, those needless criticisms on the sermon, their evil work will not be fully known until the judgment-day. If you cannot leave God's house yourself in a sober frame of mind, at least have mercy on your neighbours, and do not drive away their good thoughts by your foolish conversation. If you have found the sermon dull and tiresome, keep back your complaints of weariness; the message which has not reached you may have touched a tender chord in the heart of your companion. Your disrespectful remarks on your minister may render his labours useless, just when they were beginning to take effect. The Lord Jesus warned us that "when they have heard, Satan cometh immediately, and taketh away the word that was sown in their hearts."

This "snatching away" of the good seed at the church door and by the way-side is truly Satan's work. Who would wish to work for and with the Evil One?

Now, nothing of the sort was Augusta Berridge's desire or intention, but what mischief may we not do when we do not utter the prayers, "Cleanse thou me from secret faults," and "Set a watch, O Lord, before the door of my lips"?

There was no more true worship for little Annie that day, and when she bade Charlie goodnight, he saw that the tender, more gracious look, that had filled her countenance at church that morning was utterly gone.

Charlie had had a busy day! His Bible had been almost constantly in his hand. He had his usual reading in a course pointed out for him by mother, and then there was the Bible-class lesson, for he desired to be prepared for that.

Rev. Mayer had declared it his intention to make "the Christ of the Old Testament" the subject of his lessons, and Charlie had been puzzling over the books of Moses to find some traces of the promised Saviour. He was looking for prophecies, and was quite discouraged at discovering so few of them. But perhaps the knowledgeable Rev. Mayer could help him find more!

Charlie was very familiar with the Scriptures, and he had perhaps fancied that he should astonish Rev. Mayer by his knowledge. Yes, even Charlie Clement had his own faults, just those that naturally rose from his energetic, self-confident nature.

Rev. Mayer sat in his little study, with two candles on the table before him. Mrs. Toombs had concluded by her observations that some new plan was afoot, and when Charlie Clement rang the bell at seven o'clock, she would by no means permit her "hired girl" to go to the door. Indeed, the duty of answering the bell, Mrs. Toombs generally preferred to perform herself. She felt herself the mistress in her own castle, and so bound to look well to the outposts.

Four times the bell had rung, and four young lads appeared. Then, Mrs. Toombs was left to quiet and curiosity for the rest of the evening.

Rev. Mayer had preached from the pulpit many times, and had grown quite accustomed to it; but there was something that aroused reluctance in him at the idea of having young faces so near to him, in this homely setting. But his feeling of concern vanished when Charlie Clement came in, with his cheerful, pleasing manner, counting the other three members of the Bible-class as so many treasures, in which he was part owner.

Rev. Mayer had never felt more solemn in his life than when he knelt down with the four boys to ask the blessing of God on his new undertaking. When he closed with the Lord's Prayer, Charlie joined him, and the minister's heart thrilled with pleasure as Jack Tyler's deeper tones were heard also repeating the same words. It is hard to talk of one's mother and one's home to disinterested hearers; much harder it is to speak of Christ and heaven to unresponsive listeners. So it was cheering to Rev. Mayer to hope that at least half of his little class were ready to hear what he had to say.

At the Garden of Eden the lesson began. Rev. Mayer made the boys mark all the description of its beauty that is given, and then turn to the description of that second garden of bliss, promised in the book of Revelation to those who follow Jesus.

How were Adam and Eve, when driven from Paradise, to hope to walk by the river of the Water of Life, and eat of the fruit of that tree whose leaves are for the healing of the nations?

The promise given to our first parents sprang to Charlie's lips, and Rev. Mayer's smile told him he was right, as he recited:

"The seed of the woman shall bruise the serpent's head, which means that the Son of God shall triumph over the devil." (Genesis 3:15, 1 John 3:8).

That Christ, suffering for sinners, might have been made known to Adam, Charlie had never thought; and when Rev. Mayer dwelt upon Abel's offering of a lamb, and Adam and Eve knowing their son's sacrifice to be a sign of the coming Redeemer, Charlie's eye brightened and he exclaimed,

"O, how beautiful! I like to think of that. I have always been so sorry for Adam!"

"We all try an experiment somewhat like the one through which Adam passed. That is, we find out for ourselves that we cannot stand temptation. No one is ready to give himself up wholly to Christ, to be redeemed and sanctified, till he feels, like Adam, that he deserves to be driven from Paradise and shut out by the angel with the flaming sword," said Rev. Mayer.

Jack's eyes were fixed on the speaker, but Charlie's were cast down. Had he ever fully realized that he was utterly unworthy of salvation? The question was not to leave him at once, but would abide in his heart, demanding a full answer.

Rev. Mayer had resolved that the Bible-class should have but a short meeting. The hour he had fixed upon had passed, yet no one looked pleased when the minister's Bible was closed and the lesson was over. Even Harry and Joseph had been intellectually interested; but Jack and Charlie had felt their souls moved and enlightened. So sweetly rose the hymn that closed their exercises that Mrs. Toombs stole into the hall to catch its sounds, and even the passers-by on the streets below owned it a most welcome melody on a Sabbath evening.

Chapter 7

Homeless

Three weeks had passed pleasantly away for Rev. Mayer. He was getting better acquainted with his people. At Katy Brown's cottage he was a frequent visitor; with Jack Tyler he had many pleasant talks by the way concerning the Saviour, all of which were listened to with care. Charlie Clement was giving his minister the sunshine of his warm affection, and more than one friendly hand was reached out to the minister in his daily walks.

Saturday night had come, and full of thankfulness, Rev. Mayer had gone to rest. But his sleep was not to be uninterrupted. At midnight he was roused by the cry of "Fire!" – and by the sudden flashing of red light upon his window, it was clear, yes – fire, in all its terrors, was near his door. Hastily dressing himself, he ran to the scene of desolation and distress. Mrs. Toombs' house was one of a row of low, wooden buildings that were crowded together along the main street of Meedville. Even the most remote of these dwellings was now in flames. The cry that roused the minister had fallen on the ears of many of his people, and a crowd had already gathered, a helpless crowd, without an engine or an adequate supply of buckets.

Some effort was made to subdue the flames, but the pressing immediate necessity was to save the inhabitants from a miserable death, and only afterwards to secure some of their property before it was too late. Rev. Mayer was foremost among those who plunged his body amidst fire, smoke and falling timbers, to seek out children and aged sleepers, and to save the few belongings of the sufferers.

So rapidly the fire moved on that Mrs. Toombs' house was in danger before the fire had consumed the building where it originated. Confused and terrified, the poor woman could do nothing but hold fast to her silver spoons and cry out for help. Rev. Mayer calmly lent his aid, and saw to it that a portion of her furniture was removed, until all was too late. The roof fell in at last with a crash.

Rev. Mayer had few earthly treasures, yet his books were precious to him. In his eagerness to save those who were in danger, and to help the distressed widow with whom he had made his home, he had forgotten his books.

Now a cheerful voice at his side exclaimed, "Your books are safe, Rev. Mayer. I looked after them as soon as I saw how the fire was spreading. They are all moved to our house!" Yes, it was Charlie Clement who bestowed the joy of that moment! And so he also enjoyed the hearty "Thank you! Thank you, Charlie!" that followed.

There was no lack of homes for the houseless that night. Beds of straw were exchanged for beds of down, and the rich made the poor welcome. Mrs. Toombs, however, preferred to walk a mile into the country, to stay with one of her well-wishers, rather than to accept Mrs. Berridge's invitation to follow the minister to her house.

Sunday morning came: the bell announced the hour of the customary service. This was surely no day on which to omit the voice of prayer and thanksgiving. Yet Rev. Mayer was weak and weary; for his store of sermons had perished in the flames.

"What will Rev. Mayer do? He will break down, certainly," said Augusta Berridge to her mother, as she took her seat in the pew.

Mrs. Berridge bowed her head and managed to say, "We shall see," without any of the stir of a whispered conversation.

Never had Rev. Mayer so wholly lost himself in the service. The prayers he had so often spoken, came from his own lips like the free breathings of his own devotional feelings. Self was forgotten in the duty of the present moment.

The time for the sermon came. While others had been sleeping away the fatigue and excitement of the fire, Rev. Mayer had been deep in meditation and earnest in prayer. He could have stood up that day before assembled nations and opened his mouth, confident that it would be given unto him what to say in honour of his Heavenly Father.

Augusta Berridge cast her eye round the congregation as Rev. Mayer entered the pulpit. Many who had been wont to return her significant glances were now looking towards the clergyman, as if they were expecting to receive a message which it was all-important for them to hear. Charlie Clement's eyes were cast down; he was silently praying that the Spirit of God might so guide and direct the speaker that his words should be "words spoken in season," to bring much joy to many hearts.

Ah, if the critical hearers would cease to be on the watch for defects, and pray for him who is about to address them, then, indeed, might the preached word of God become a mighty engine for good.

Calmly, Rev. Mayer gave out the text – "The Son of Man had not where to lay His head." The beggarly and houseless were gathered in the church that day with those who had tenderly felt for neighbours, thrust from their homes, and families suddenly left destitute.

The Saviour, a pilgrim without a refuge, was brought before them, and every eye was fixed, every ear was ready to listen.

Jesus, the King of heaven, was once more among them, sympathizing with the distressed and cheering His true children to acts of kindness. Jesus, the ascended Lord, was calling on the homeless of earth to share His home in the skies, to ensure a place in the heavenly mansions, where sorrow cannot come.

Never had Divine truth been so preached from that pulpit! Never had those hearers so welcomed the good seed in honest hearts. There was no gossip at the church door that day. Satan snatched away no good seed by idle chat by the wayside.

Charlie handed her into the sleigh in his best style.

Chapter 8

A Fall

Christmas had showered its gifts in the lap of childhood, and breathed its whispers of sacred comfort to the more way-worn pilgrims of earth. The New Year had opened with its halo of hope and its rainbow of good resolutions.

Two months had passed since Charlie Clement left his home on a Southern plantation and came to the north to carry on the education that had been so thoroughly and wisely commenced.

His mother's kind, judicious influence no longer surrounded him like a protective mantle. The freedom he had from the faults of most boys of this age, which Charlie fancied to be the result of his own better character, was about to be sorely tested. The manliness which had been most attractive when it had developed in a son, guarding and sustaining a widowed mother, became less agreeable in the boy when he must now rule his own spirit.

The idea that he was sufficient in of his own power and strength to do all, and know all, daily increased in Charlie. Augusta made sport of him and called him "Mr. Pomposity," and Annie looked up to him as the wonder he seemed to think himself; but

Rev. Mayer saw with deep pain the change that was coming over his dear young companion. His gentle warnings to Charlie seemed to have no effect, yet he did not despair. His quiet influence might yet do something, and that he brought to bear by being much in the society of his youthful friend, who was so dear to him. Rev. Mayer really believed that Charlie was a true child of God and would not be suffered to fall prey to the temptations of one great fault. For him he prayed most fervently, yet trembled while he prayed, lest only the most severe discipline should bring back the wanderer to the humility of a follower of Jesus.

The time for the confirmation was approaching, yet Charlie was not very regular at the services the minister had appointed as preparation for that rite; he seemed to think his preparation so thorough that he needed no additional word of counsel, no closer self-examination.

A bright Saturday, early in February, had come. The snow made white the country far and wide, and the merry sleigh-bells sounded out through the streets of Meedville and over the glittering meadows. The beautiful scenes of the day made Charlie determined that he must share a ride with friends, so early that morning he engaged a sleigh and horses which suited his taste, and at two o'clock he appeared at Mrs. Berridge's door, as full of merriment as if life was all careless boyhood.

Augusta soon came out, all wrapped in furs and full of smiles. Charlie was just handing her into the sleigh, in his best style, when Mrs. Berridge's face appeared at the parlour window. The sash was thrown up in a moment and the mother exclaimed,

"Charlie! Charlie! Stop! You are not going to drive Black Fury, are you?"

"Why not? I am quite used to horses. Never fear, aunt, I know what I am about."

"But Augusta! I don't dare to trust you," began Mrs. Berridge. Charlie was by this time in his seat, and in another moment the spirited horse was galloping down the street at full speed.

Mrs. Berridge cast a long, anxious glance after the little party, and did not move from the window until the sound of bells had died upon her ear.

The keen air and the rapid motion were exhilarating! Charlie urged his horse on at headlong speed. He had entered one of the lanes near Meedville when bells were heard ringing loudly behind them.

Augusta turned her head, and exclaimed, "It is Harry DeWitt! Don't let him pass us!"

There was no danger of anyone passing Black Fury when he was excited by the sound of horses' feet behind him. On he sped, as if unconscious of the light vehicle attached to him, while Charlie vainly endeavoured to rein him in.

They were now beyond the beaten road, and Charlie knew not which way to steer among the snowdrifts and gulleys which extended from fence to fence.

Black Fury plunged madly on, for the sleigh was but a plaything to the strong horse in his excitement. Taking a bend at great speed, the sleigh tipped over, but the frantic horse slowed his pace not a bit, even with the sleigh fallen on its side, cutting through the snow, with both riders getting a face full! Soon all came to a halt and Augusta found herself lodged in a bed of snow. It would have been happy for Charlie if he had found as soft a resting-place, but his arm had caught in the reins as the sleigh went over, and with it he was dragged along, now dashed against the runners, whirling through the snow, his body plowing it as he passed. The reins broke at last, and Charlie was left dumbstruck and senseless by the road-side.

Harry DeWitt took Augusta into his sleigh with some pride; he was not unwilling to have a little triumph over Charlie, who was particularly proud of his skill as a "whip."

Harry had no idea of following the mad course of the Black Fury, now free to run without restraint in the lanes. "I ought not to risk Miss Augusta's life in such a chase," he said to himself; but with a feeling of regret at not being able to do more, he turned his horse's head back towards Meedville to deliver the girl to her home.

Charlie was not to lack a friend in his troubles. Jack Tyler had been out with his wood-sled, and had just turned a corner which led to the lane in which Charlie had driven, when the maddened horse dashed past him. Jack did not stop to pursue the horse, for he felt sure that this was a sign he was more needed in the contrary direction. On he went, plodding as fast as he could through the deep snow.

Charlie did not know whose strong arms were folded tenderly around him. He did not see the honest face that was wet with tears as it bent over him. He could not know that eager observers appeared at the windows as he was carried through Meedville, as helpless a burden as the wood upon which he was laid. Very different were his feelings now, upon his rescue in that humble sled, from those at his departure, so full of pride and excitement.

Charlie was restored to consciousness to find his body racked with pain and stiff in every limb. He knew his aunt was not fond of nursing; he knew it was costly to her stout figure to be exerted so; yet he had no choice, she must wait upon him now, and to know that it was his own folly that had made him a burden to her was a grief to him. Even the keeper of the livery-stable had warned him against the horse he had chosen to drive, yet he had presumptuously risked his own life and that of his friend. But they had both been spared! O that thought! Charlie dwelt upon it with deep gratitude, but gratitude mingled with bitter repentance. In the silence of his sick room a hideous sight seemed to rise before his mind's eye, a sight from which he would have gladly turned away his gaze. It was himself, full of presumption and self-importance, and he was sick at heart. Where was the modesty that is becoming in youth? Where was the humility, without which piety must become an empty word?

Charlie Clement saw himself, and he was humbled in dust and ashes; but, blessed be God, when our eyes are opened to behold our own sinfulness, He pours into them the light of His Sun of Righteousness, and comforts His children with this vision of mercy and redeeming love.

Now came the faithful words of a friend. Rev. Mayer did not say "Peace! Peace!" until he was sure that the arrow of heaven had pierced even to the depths of the soul. He brought home the rebuke that was needed, before he poured in the oil of consolation.

Charlie had learned this lesson: that no religious habits, no faithful training, will alone guarantee that a young Christian is kept from sin. He falls when exposed to temptation, unless watching with prayer, and upheld by the power of his Father in heaven. Charlie's fall might seem a little matter to onlookers, but he knew himself how far he had wandered from the true spirit of a follower of Christ. Humble as a little child, he lay in his sick room, while others were to enjoy the privilege of openly professing themselves servants of the Lord Jesus at the confirmation service.

A day later, while Charlie lay healing in bed, the church at Meedville was crowded. Many had come merely as spectators to the confirmation service; but many more arrived as devout worshippers. The minister stood in the chapel as the persons to be confirmed were called on to come forward. A sunburnt youth, whose broad shoulders proved him familiar with toil, walked slowly up the aisle. No faltering thought, no fear of man, slackened his usual bold, firm tread. He moved gently, to keep pace with the aged woman who leaned on his arm.

Poor and coarsely clad, was Katy Brown. There was no charm in her dark and wrinkled features, yet at her Rev. Mayer looked tenderly and anxiously, as she drew near. In that worn and weary body was an immortal soul, a soul that he brought into the fullness of the gospel light. Yes, that aged woman was the first fruits of Marshall Mayer's ministry, and he rejoiced over her with great joy. Jack he had guided and directed, but to Katy, it had been his blessed privilege to declare the truth as it is in Jesus, and to see it become precious to her heart.

Who can describe the devout interest of the faithful pastor as he prayed for her in the words, "Defend, O Lord, this Thy servant, with Thy heavenly grace, that she may continue Thine forever, and daily increase in Thy Holy Spirit more and more, until she come unto Thine everlasting kingdom."

For Jack there might yet be a hard struggle, a battle for his soul with temptation; but the old pilgrim Katy was near her journey's end. She had but the dark valley to pass, and she would enter into the reward purchased for the penitent by the blood of Jesus.

O, the riches of the mercy of Christ! Who would not enlist under this Captain of our salvation? Who would not labour in the vineyard of such a gracious Lord?

Chapter 9

Annie's Work

"It is almost worth having been shut up so long, for the reward of being so glad to be with you all again," said Charlie Clement, with one of those familiar, bright smiles again on his face.

The family circle upon which Charlie looked was indeed a cheerful one. Gathered about the centre-table sat Mrs. Berridge, Augusta, and Annie, each as busy as if convinced that industry was the secret of happiness. Mrs. Berridge was knitting an afghan, and the portion of her completed work lay across her lap, its gay stripes seeming the brighter for the brilliant gas-light that fell upon them. Mrs. Berridge was just one of those ladies who seemed most in her place when sitting in her own parlour, occupied about some pretty work. There was a quiet, settled look in her stout figure, and a sort of repose in her face, that made one feel rested to look at her.

Augusta, on the contrary, was all animation. When her mouth opened, her blue eyes sparkled and did their part to enhance the vivacious expression of her face. Augusta was drawing, handling her pencil with a skill that made it a pleasure to watch her.

Charlie took up the spirited head of Apollo, which she was just finishing, and gave it the glance of a connoisseur. He was about to hazard some criticisms, and to make some mythological allusions that were more calculated to show his own powers than to please the hearers, when there was a whisper at his heart that checked him. With a well-deserved compliment on her work, he handed it back to Augusta, who took it with a laugh and said,

"I think Mr. Pomposity died in your sick room. Do you think that one of the Siamese twins will be able to live without the other, eh, Charlie?"

"I hope so," said Charlie, sobered by this unexpected remark.

"You ought not to call Charlie names," said Annie, looking protectively at her cousin.

"You need not stand to your arms on all occasions, Annie, when Charlie is spoken to," said Augusta, not very pleasantly.

"Annie and I are firm friends," said Charlie, with a fond look at his little cousin. "Come, Annie, let me see your work?"

Annie thrust her hands under the table. Her work was not truly such as would please an artist's eye. She was embroidering on a piece of brown broadcloth such flowers as no botanist could have recognized; even the leaves were of angular forms, which might be sought for in vain in nature.

Annie was a happy, comfortable, tender-hearted little girl of ten, but by no means sensitive. Charlie could not account for the sudden bashfulness that had overtaken her. So, after his persistent request, she finally exhibited her work and reluctantly owned that she was making a watch-case.

"A watch-case!" said Augusta, with a laugh. "I thought it was a bag for some baby's silver porringer, or perhaps a bowl for some worthy potato, to which a small specimen of the same kind had grown fat. Who is it for, I pray?"

"Let me see if it will fit," said Charlie, taking out his watch and slipping it into the case.

"The watch is like truth, hid in a well," said Augusta. "It can't be for you, Charlie, so draw your watch up from the depths."

"Don't say any more about it, Charlie," whispered Annie, beseechingly.

"Who will go and get my books for me?" said Charlie. "I am in a studying mood."

Annie hastened to oblige her cousin, while Augusta laughingly said,

"I wonder that Mrs. Toombs allows Rev. Mayer to come here to hear you recite. I don't think she has ever forgiven us for keeping him that whole fortnight after the fire. She is a peculiar lady. I wonder what such people were made for?"

"Made to do some particular good work, no doubt," said Charlie. "But here come my books, and I must go to studying in earnest."

Charlie had never studied so faithfully as since Rev. Mayer had kindly offered to act as his tutor until he should be able to reappear at the academy. Charlie's perfect recitations left time enough during the appointed hour for much that was interesting in the way of explanations. Often the hour closed with a pleasant, profitable talk between the minister and his young parishioner, which was to have its impression when the things of this world have passed away.

Chapter 10

Annie's Visit

The fire which had burned Rev. Mayer's sermons, and left him without a home, had been by no means an enemy. The sermons that he had laboured over at the seminary, or wrought out in his study since his arrival at Meedville, had been profitable to his mind, by way of discipline; but with them his heart had little to do. They were fit for the fire; like a boy's old Latin exercises, they had fulfilled their end and were to be cast aside for better things.

Rev. Mayer now knew his people. He loved them, he felt for their wants, and to them he spoke when he entered the pulpit, for it was now for their sakes that he wrote in his study. The people, likewise, knew that they were being directly addressed by a friend who had their best interest at heart, and they listened and took home his earnest appeals and faithful counsel.

Members of the town who had thought little of their minister or his home, had their sympathies called out towards him when his wardrobe was burnt, his study furniture destroyed, and he was forced to accept the kind invitation of Mrs. Berridge to make her house his home.

Mrs. Toombs soon found a house placed at her disposal as well, at an uncommonly low rent, and found other hands than hers interested in providing for the minister's comfort.

No one acknowledged who had placed the new suits in his bedroom closet. No one claimed the credit of newly furnishing the study. Stout farmers and country shop-keepers who had given themselves no concern about their minister when he was comfortable, had found pleasure in relieving him in his unexpected difficulties. They knew what they had done, and they felt an added interest in one for whom they were able to do something.

And Mrs. Berridge – had she no part in this work of love? Apparently none; yet Rev. Mayer received through the post-office a blank envelope containing a fifty dollar bill; it seemed to him likely that this was an act of her generosity.

These nameless kindnesses made Rev. Mayer feel that he was among friends, and his stiffness gave way to a frank and kindly manner that strengthened the pleasant relations growing up between him and his people.

Rev. Mayer was sitting in his study one morning in April when there was a timid ring at the door. Mrs. Toombs was at her post in a moment; motioning back the "hired girl" who was peeping after her round the corner of the entry, the little woman opened the door. There stood Annie

Berridge, looking no means as calm and comfortable as usual.

"Is Rev. Mayer at home?" asked the little girl.

"Yes. What would you have me tell him, child?" said Mrs. Toombs, standing before Annie.

Annie fumbled nervously at a little parcel in her hand, and the repeated her question.

"Is Rev. Mayer at home?"

Mrs. Toombs tended to be suspicious of any conversation between her lodger and Mrs. Berridge's family. She seemed to have conceived a vague notion that there was a plan to decoy him away, which it was her duty to check in the bud. She now looked at the parcel most curiously, and said, "Shall I give it to him?"

Annie was about to render up, helplessly, her treasure, when Rev. Mayer himself appeared. And it would have been a great disappointment to Annie to have to go away without an interview, and so her face grew quite bright at the sight of her minister's face.

"Come in, Annie, how do you do this morning?" he said, kindly taking her hand. The air was chilly and there was a cheerful wood fire on the study-hearth. "Come and warm your fingers," said Rev. Mayer, drawing Annie towards the bright flame.

Mrs. Toombs fidgeted uneasily, but retreated down the hall at length, without even speaking to the "hired girl," who was still at her post of observation.

"I made this for your watch."

It seemed to take Annie a great while to warm her hands. She held them up before the fire long after they were perfectly comfortable. The package had been hastily thrust into her pocket. She had given a most minute and satisfactory account on the health of all her family before she could make up her mind to begin the ceremony of presentation. As to this moment, she had given much thought and had planned precisely what she would say; now, however, all her intended remarks had forsaken her and she could only stammer out,

"I made this for your watch, and so I have come to bring it."

Rev. Mayer unfolded the little parcel and took out the result of Annie's labours. Such a watch-case had not often been seen, yet Rev. Mayer looked at it with as much pleasure as if it were an exquisite work of art. He knew that love had prompted the gift, making this gift precious in a degree that the finest craftsmanship could never match.

Affection was all the more welcome to Rev. Mayer, because he had been so long alone in the world, a mere student, without a family circle or a home. Affection he prized for its own sake; he moreover knew that if he wished to lead his young parishioners heavenward, they must place their hands lovingly and trustfully in his.

Now, he looked very kindly at Annie as he thanked her for her gift.

"See, how nicely it fits," he said, as he placed his great silver watch in the case. "You could not have done better if you had taken its measurements!"

Annie looked curiously at the watch and Rev. Mayer put it in her hand. The watch was covered with deep carvings and was as thick as two watches, such as are now made.

"This was my grandfather's watch," said Rev. Mayer, opening it and showing the works. Annie watched the silent motion of the wheels, while Rev. Mayer went on to say,

"So it went, tick, tick, when my good grandfather was alive. His wonderful body wore out and was laid in the grave, yet here the watch is going, going still. Does a watch then last longer than a man?"

Annie looked up suddenly as she answered,

"Yes! I mean, no! Well, in a kind of way!"

"It lasts longer than a man's body, but the watch has no soul to live forever, even when it is worn out," said Rev. Mayer. "It is only made for use in this world. Yet how carefully we use it, what pains we take lest it should be injured. Is not a soul worth as much trouble? It needs to be guarded and kept from harm, too; but does it not need something more?"

"It needs to be made better," said Annie, modestly.

"Yes, it needs to be placed in Jesus' hands to be made pure, and kept in the right way, here on earth, and then it will be His in the happy home in heaven. Does not Jesus hear when children pray, Annie?"

"I suppose so; but it seems as if He could not understand what children want, as He does grown-up people."

"Dear little Annie, you know that Jesus was once a child. You remember very well what happened yesterday. Jesus never forgets, He cannot forget. He remembers as well now when He was a little boy at Nazareth, as you do what you saw and heard but a moment ago. He knows what it is to live in a child's body and to have a child's troubles. He had parents to obey and young companions to make happy. He has not forgotten a child's feelings. He can sympathize with you, when no one else can. You must learn to love Him and to go to Him in all your joys and troubles."

As Rev. Mayer closed, Annie looked up earnestly into his face and said, with a great effort, three simple words – "I am trying." Three simple words they were, yet they filled the heart of the minister with pure joy. Poor little Annie! It cost her such a struggle to make this confession, that her eyes flowed out suddenly with tears. It was, to her, a profession of Christ – her first owning to any human being that she wanted to have Him for her Master. Rev. Mayer knelt down with the little girl, and spoke for her to the loving Saviour, who understood this child, having once been a child.

When Annie went forth from that room, it was with the pleasant thought that Jesus was to be with her by the way-side and in her home.

Chapter 11

A Black Shadow

Farmer Watkins' eyes were heavy with sleep; he was, for once, weary – not with working, but with watching. He could have borne harvesting labours, even with only a single hand to help him, better than this standing by a sick-bed day and night. "A woman's business, this" he said it was; and yet it was plain his heart was in it.

Farmer Watkins was a bachelor and not much in the habit of looking out for other people's comfort; but there was one man living on his place who had managed to get a hold upon him which triumphed over selfishness. Farmer Watkins loved and respected Jack Tyler, and he could not bear to see him stretched out on a sick-bed without it causing many a pang in his own soul. Jack had been seized with a malignant fever; two days and nights his employer had been at his side, nursing him as tenderly as was possible to a man of his rough hands and even rougher ways.

Now night was settling over the farm-house, and sleep soon began to take an equally firm hold on the farmer's watchfulness. He paced the room, shook himself, reminding himself of the medicines to be given Jack at every hour through the night. He looked at Jack, tossing and murmuring strange nonsense, as the fever affected him. "No! This cannot be! The good fellow should have proper care," and with stern determination in his face, the farmer took his seat beside him. His eyes, notwithstanding his resolutions, were beginning to droop, when there was a rap at the outer door. A hand soon beckoned the farmer from his post.

Rev. Mayer was in the hall below. He had come, he said, to pass the night with Jack. Farmer Watkins looked at the minister and exclaimed, "It's catchin', the fever is! You are worth too much to be took down that way. No, no! I can stand it out a good piece longer on my own."

The farmer felt very wide awake now, in the fresh air of the hall, but when, a half hour afterwards, he lay on his own bed, he slept as if he was in a trance, his deep snores being heard throughout the house like the sounding of trumpets.

Through the weary night hours sat Rev. Mayer by the bed of Jack Tyler. The sufferer knew a gentle hand ministered to him, and now and then a strange glance of a half-puzzled recognition lighted up his features.

Those ravings, those muttered words of delirium, were poor companionship in the midnight hour; yet even in them the minister found comfort. They were but the upturning of a mind where evil had been allowed no resting-place, and habits of sin were strangers. Jack had fallen into a quiet doze, when, in the gray dawn, the farmer appeared at the door. Refreshed by his night's sleep, he realized all the more the kindness of the "friend in need" who had relieved him at his post, and his thanks abundantly expressed his appreciation of the service which had been rendered to him.

A messenger on horseback had come with a summons for Rev. Mayer. The same fever that had prostrated the strong woodsman, Jack Tyler, and had closed forever the eyes of old Katy Brown, had now filled Augusta Berridge's veins with fire! Augusta's mind, it was reported, still had power to think and reason; which only rendered more fearful the agony she endured – agony both of body and mind. Her present sufferings brought before her a faint image of what might be in store for her soul – that soul to which she had given so little thought in her days of health. And was her mother a guide and comforter to her little girl, in this time of distress? Alas, for Mrs. Berridge, no! For she knew not the Heavenly Father, and so had no comfort for her daughter, groping in a horror of great darkness. She knew not the way to the foot of the cross; like Augusta, she was but beginning to seek that which she should have sought first, "the kingdom of heaven and its righteousness."

Again and again, in Augusta's sick-room, Rev. Mayer had lifted up the voice of prayer. Where duty called, Marshall Mayer would go, though with every breath he might take in a fatal disease. So now he urged his horse onward, as he hastened to the saddened home of Mrs. Berridge.

Annie noiselessly opened the door, and Charlie silently extended a hand to him in the hall. To the bedside of the suffering girl he was promptly led. At his first observation of her, his thought was, "Where is the sparkling vivacity that had so distinguished Augusta Berridge a few short weeks before?" Sad, sunken eyes gazed forth from her thin, pale face, and no words of sarcastic mirth came from her parched lips. Yet those lips were suddenly able to cry, "God be merciful to me, a sinner!" – and those sad cyes were lifted to heaven.

Rev. Mayer knew that he was in the presence of a soul trembling on the brink of eternity; and Oh how tenderly, how faithfully he pictured the blessed Jesus, coming to seek and to save this one that was lost. How, like a child drawing near to a father, he drew near to God, asking His best blessings of mercy for her who was so earnestly desiring pardon and forgiveness.

Would the Saviour stoop to one sinner more, and lift her soul from the dust? Would Augusta Berridge be raised up to serve her Maker?

Who can tell the issues of life and death? Who knows, lying down at evening, if he will rise in the morning? Who knows when this body we cherish and guard will sicken and die, and then the neglected soul be called to account before God?

This we do know: "God waiteth to be gracious," and to all He says, "Now is the accepted time, now is the day of salvation."

Chapter 12

Purer Air

Meedville had been considered one of those healthy places, where it is of no use for young doctors to settle. There was no part of the quiet, country town given up to wickedness and filth, or habits that fostered disease and death.

Now and then an infant was laid in its quiet tomb, like a flower dropping on the bosom of mother earth. Now and then a hoary head drooped, as the ripened seed, and like that seed, was planted to rise on the resurrection morn.

Occasionally some young, fair girl, or a man in the fullness of his strength, was called to lie down and die, as if to say, in words too startling to be mistaken, "Watch, therefore, for ye know not the day or the hour when the Son of Man cometh." So it had been at Meedville, since the now white-haired settlers made for themselves, in their youth, a home in the wilderness. No pestilence had ever prevailed in the favoured spot; and but for his own independent income, the slow-moving, cheerful-looking old doctor would have had to give up his profession, and devote himself to some more money-making business.

The sudden appearance of a malignant, contagious fever among them had struck the people of Meedville with a fearful panic. The stout-hearted failed in this time of need; and there were more willing to take the easy path and flee from the scene of contagion, than to stand by the bedsides of the sufferers with the patient tenderness of a skilful nurse.

It was at this time that Marshall Mayer moved among the sick and dying, to soothe their pain-racked bodies and comfort sin-sick souls. He had no near relations to mourn his loss; no home would be left desolate if he were taken away. Perhaps these circumstances made it easier for him to peril his life where others dared not to go; but the great well-spring of his courage was his deep conviction that death could have no terrors for him, for his Lord had died.

The friends who gather round us in health, and add their joy to ours, are dear; but dearer are those who come to us when sickness makes dreary the family hearth and silences the voice of mirth. Ah! How we prize the friend that comes like a sister to relieve the worn-out nurses, and give the sufferer a placid face to look upon, not yet marked with the weariness of long watching! How we welcome the manly form that can bow at the sick-bed with a woman's tenderness, yet lends its strength, like a rock, for the helpless to rest upon!

Years of ordinary ministry might have done less to endear Marshall Mayer to his people than did those few, dark, dark weeks, when fever hung round the town like a plague. The villagers could not but love the friend who had been their human stay in their time of trouble, and had taught them where to seek for a support that would not fail them when called to go through the deep waters of affliction, or to enter the valley of the shadow of death. Rev. Mayer's regular, temperate life, and his vigorous constitution, had prepared him to endure great fatigue. Though Mrs. Toombs daily fretted at his exposing his valuable life, and daily expected to see him laid upon a sick-bed of his own, he did only grow a little paler and thinner. The good woman at length ceased her murmurings and instead spent her energies in preparing cooling drinks for fevered lips and nourishing food for the convalescents.

Health once more began to throb in Jack Tyler's veins. Augusta Berridge, too, was coming back to life, looking like a rising shadow, but healing nonetheless. Jack was rising up to be doubly pledged to a life of usefulness, and Augusta thought her soul as much changed as her poor body. Her soul was truly changed! It was now her chief wish and purpose to obey and serve her Heavenly Father, rather than follow the evil promptings of her own nature. This change had taken place, but Augusta of course had her natural character to struggle with, her wrong habits to overcome. She had a work before her that could only be accomplished by watchfulness and prayer.

The cloud seemed to have passed away from Meedville, and many hearts were full of gratitude. White slabs had suddenly clustered among moss-grown stones of the graveyard, and mourning garments had taken the place of gay attire; yet the scourge had proved a blessing, and "the Lord and Giver of life" had written many new names in His book of remembrance.

Chapter 13

A Vestry Meeting

The year for which Rev. Mayer had been engaged to supply the pulpit at Meedville had passed. Mrs. Toombs was restless and uneasy; but Charlie Clement was confident that his wishes were to be realized. The vestry held their meeting; the very children in the street would have reproached them had their decision been other than it was.

Who should they have for their pastor? Who would so care for their souls as the dear friend who had not hesitated to risk his life on their behalf? They knew who was welcome when the spirit saw eternity opening before it. They knew who could wipe away the mourner's tear and whisper words of consolation. They knew who could win the hearts of their little ones and lead them to Jesus. The meeting of the vestry was but an occasion for expressing the rejoicing that Rev. Mayer could be retained among them. As with once voice they declared it their belief that God had greatly blessed them in sending one to labour among them who was such a faithful follower of his gracious Lord. Rev. Mayer's long years of loneliness had not deadened his heart to affection, and when his people, with a spontaneous movement, waited upon him to express their attachment, and to beg him to remain among them, his heart was so warmed and touched that his lips refused to speak, but his moistened eyes, for a moment, gave answer; and then he broke forth in the touching words of Ruth: "This people shall be my people, and their God my God; and the Lord do so to me, and more also, if anything but death part them and me!"

And did the people of Meedville fancy they had secured perfection in their minister? No, they knew him to be a man of like passions to themselves, heir of the same corruption, redeemed by the same Saviour, being one gradually sanctified by the same Spirit. And who but one like this, who understood that he likewise struggled against sin, could feel for those who are tempted? Who better than a sinner, clinging himself to the cross of Christ, could point out to the despairing the only sure refuge? Who but one "bought with a price" himself could devote himself body, soul, and spirit, to the work of his Heavenly Master?

Of our Saviour it is said, "Wherefore in all things it behooved him to be made like unto his brethren, that He might be a merciful and faithful high priest, in all things pertaining to God, to make reconciliation for the sins of the people. For in that He Himself hath suffered being tempted, He is able to succour them that are tempted." If even the Lord Jesus took humanity upon Himself that He might be our compassionate Redeemer, we need not wonder that no perfect men are sent among us as our ministers. God chooses in the midst of weakness to show His strength. To those who lean wholly upon Him in the fulfillment of their high commission, He gives a power to become holy and a might to minister in His service that redounds all the more to His honour for the weakness of the instrument employed. The people of Meedville had found no perfect being, but they had been blessed with the services of a true, conscientious, devout Christian man. He was their ordained and instituted guide in the heavenly way. To him they meant to give not a pittance, but an abundant support; not criticism and opposition, but confidence and co-operation. They would join him in his prayers, hear him in his sermons, and honour him by obedience to his counsel.

Chapter 14

A Visit Home

Charlie Clement was going home for his vacation. Home! His very heart leaped at the word. Dearer than ever was his mother now to him, and he longed to be once more at her side. Mingled with all this joy was much regret at leaving Meedville, even for a short time. There were now many ties to bind him to his aunt's family circle, to his dear minister, and to the church, where he had first come forward to commemorate his Saviour's love.

Meedville would ever be dear to him, a place around which the most delightful associations would cluster.

"We shall all miss you sadly. I never had any idea before what a comfort a son might be to a widowed mother," said Mrs. Berridge, fondly.

"I can't bear to let you go," said Annie, drawing closer to her cousin in her affectionate way. "I liked you at first, but lately you seem nicer – not so old, somehow."

"We must become as little children if we would enter the kingdom of heaven," said Rev. Mayer, who was enjoying the last hour of Charlie's stay with him.

"Yes!" said Charlie, earnestly, and his heart was full of humble joy. No parting gift could have been so precious to Charlie as Annie's heartfelt words. Had he then triumphed, to a degree, over his besetting sin?! The thought was a spring to renewed efforts to seek that humility which is the crowning grace of the young Christian.

Mrs. Berridge was at this moment called out of the room. The visitor was no other than Mrs. Toombs, who modestly refused to enter the house farther than the dining-room. She no longer looked on Mrs. Berridge as her natural enemy, and had said, in her own queer way, "I was all wrong to want nobody to take care of Rev. Mayer but me. The more friends he has, the better, I say now."

This morning she had come with a basket of choice sandwiches for "Mr. Charlie to eat on the way, and to wish him good luck, as the warmest hearted boy that ever came to Meedville."

When Mrs. Berridge urged her to give her message to Charlie in person, she shrunk back in dismay and abruptly disappeared. Mrs. Toombs was still Mrs. Toombs, though profiting by the labours of her much-respected minister.

Mrs. Berridge returned to the parlour and gave the basket and message to Charlie. Very welcome they both were to him.

"I like her, and I thank her," said Charlie. "We can't all be the same. Variety is the spice of life."

Augusta was going to hazard one of her old sharp remarks about Mrs. Toombs. "But we don't want pepper in puddings, or Mrs. Toombs' peculiarities in a woman," she was thinking to say; but she changed her mind and stayed silent. For Augusta had learned something about the unruly member – her tongue – and was trying harder now to govern it, in obedience to her Lord.

"Have you everything ready, Charlie?" said Mrs. Berridge, with a motherly, anxious look.

Charlie did not resent the questioning of his skills as a traveler, but held up the cap in his hand, saying, "I have only this to put on, Aunt!"

"And that you will have to do at once, for here is the hack at the door," said Augusta. "You have been a real good cousin to me, and I can't bear to spare you," she added in a lower voice. "Your example has meant a great deal to me!"

Annie had to let go her hold upon her cousin, and all the good-byes had to come to an end, for the cars would not wait, and the slow hack-horses must have full time allowed them.

"I am so glad I shall have you here when I come back," said Charlie to Rev. Mayer when they were seated in the hack.

"And I am glad you are coming back," replied Rev. Mayer. "I have never told you, Charlie, how your bright young face broke in upon my studies, and changed this mere student into something like a pastor. Your visit was a real heart-warming to me. I shall miss you sadly."

"And what have you not done for me?" said Charlie, earnestly, "poor, self-important boy that I was. If I ever am the humble Christian I want to be, I shall have to thank you for setting me on my guard against my pride."

"Dear Charlie, every character has its own peculiar faults, to be struggled against with watchfulness and prayer. I will not speak of mine; but I must say that a loving, earnest young Christian may do much for his minister, in his inner work, as well as his outward labours. God bless you, my boy, and sustain you in all your temptations until we meet again."

Very affectionate was the parting between Rev. Mayer and Charlie. Away went the happy lad to his mother and his home; and back returned the minister to his well-beloved parish.

We need no prophet's eye to trace their future course. Each went on as he began. Charlie continued, a faithful, active, affectionate servant of Christ. Taking his heart in hand, he devoted his all to the service of his Maker, and ever remained, to his minister, the same tried and trusted friend; freely giving his sympathy and aid in every perplexity and every good work.

The Rev. Marshall Mayer likewise followed closely after the footsteps of his Divine Master. For the bodies as well as the souls of his people, did he feel a tender interest. In their temporal trials, as in their spiritual needs, he was their comforter and best adviser.

To him the hoary head looked up, and his hand led little children in the paths of righteousness.

He did not sink under the responsibilities of his office. Cheerfully, hopefully, he went forward. Trusting in the Captain of his salvation, year after year he comes off victorious. For him will be laid up a crown of rejoicing, when he shall appear in the kingdom of the redeemed. For him will sound the welcome at the gates of the heavenly city.

The End

Ears For Little Gleaners

by

Herbert Dawson

~ *with numerous illustrations* ~

Preface

Every parent who feels the realities of eternity has an anxiety of soul over his dear children, as we behold the evil days in which we live; it makes us solemn regarding their future.

I have spent many wonderful hours addressing boys and girls in our church. My desire and aim has always been to store their youthful minds with good counsel for life and sound teaching from the Bible. I have been especially anxious to show these dear young friends the unspeakable importance of "the new birth," for "ye must be born again."

The fruits of morality may be found upon a tree not planted in righteousness. But when real Christian faith takes root in one's heart, it bears fruits in lip and life which excel the mere fruits of "morality" by as much as the sun at noon outshines a candle. The fruits of morality can only benefit in this life, "but godliness is profitable unto all things, having the promise of the life that now is, and of that which is to come."

So, I have named this book "Ears for Little Gleaners," for I have sought to sow seed that may result in a harvest of life for the young – "ears" of counsel, "ears" of warning, "ears" of exhortation and "ears" of sound doctrine.

O may the God of truth deign to bless this little book and the dear young friends who may read it.

~ Herbert Dawson ~

Friendly Words to Fathers and Mothers

O what a solemn responsibility rests upon a father and mother to "train up a child in the way he should go" (Prov. 22:6). The little folk who sit around our tables and play about the house give us many anxious thoughts when we think of the dangers on the path of life which they are just commencing to tread. And when we think of the tremendous fact that our children are hastening to an eternal goal – heaven or hell – Oh, what searchings of heart a godly parent feels, and how such exercises lead to the Psalmist's prayer: "Let Thy work appear unto Thy servants, and Thy glory unto their children" (Psalm 90:16).

I feel it requires special grace and wisdom to train up a child in the way he should go. I have been much impressed by the injunctions in the Word of God concerning the obligations which fall upon fathers and mothers. The children of Israel were enjoined: "When thou buildest a new house, then thou shalt make a battlement for thy roof." An Eastern house-top was flat, and served as a garden, a resting-place, a play-ground for the children, and many other useful purposes. Thus, a surrounding fence – called a "battlement" – was necessary to prevent people falling from the roof.

May not these "battlements" set forth the rules, and principles, and teaching, which a faithful parent will build around his household to prevent his children falling into many dangerous snares?

The Apostle Paul urges, "Bring them up in the nurture and admonition of the Lord." And this will be a great concern of heart to a godly parent. As the husbandmen ties the plant to the stake, training it upward, even so the children should be trained in a right way and fastened to the stake of righteousness by loving ties of parental affection. The law said to the fathers and mothers in Israel: "And these words, which I command thee this day, shall be in thine heart: and thou shalt teach them diligently unto thy children." The meaning of this word for "teach" is to "sharpen" or "whet," and conveys the idea of sharpening, as with a scythe – a reminder to parents to continually sharpen the minds of their children in the knowledge of what is right and wrong.

The most important method of teaching is by example. It is vain for parents to enforce precepts and principles which they do not keep themselves, and live in daily life. If the command "train up a child in the way he should go" is to be carried out, the parent must be in that way himself, and lead the child therein by a daily example of right principles in the path of life.

A parent should watch three important things in children – the tongue, the hands, and the feet.

1st, the Tongue. Idle words, exaggerated statements, frivolity, falsehood, and wrong speeches should be checked and corrected. It is a sad sight to see boys and girls who are beyond parental discipline, and who answer back and disobey, doing as they like. A solemn harvest will be reaped by such parents, and too late, the folly of not keeping children under right government will be seen.

2nd, the Hands. It should be a "law of the house" not to be altered, to allow no novels, poisonous books, and harmful things in the hands of children. The hand which takes the forbidden lump of sugar from the basin must be checked. A little thief may imbibe habits of dishonesty and bring sad havoc to a parent's home and heart. And the hand which strikes the angry blow must be checked also.

3rd, the Feet. We live in days when children are allowed great latitude as to what they do and where they go; but the Word of God is the same. Can a godly parent allow his child to go where sinners abound? An honest conscience must answer "No!" The children of modern days will call such a method of training strait-laced, narrow-minded, and old-fashioned, but let every father and mother stick to the Word of God. "Train up a child in the way he should go." The Word of God is old-fashioned, and woe be to the parent who departs from its laws.

If home-life was made what it should be, how many youths and maidens would be preserved from going out into worldly society to obtain so-called pleasures. Lawful pleasures should be provided by all fathers and mothers who value the happiness of family life. What are lawful pleasures? Among them are, good books for the children to read; music and singing in the home; edifying and instructive conversation; country rambles; many helpful studies in the world in which we live; profitable hobbies and occupations; and a thousand other things which lead to the fulfillment of the great commandments, to "love the Lord thy God with all thy heart, and with all thy soul, and with all thy mind" and to "love thy neighbour as thyself."

It should be a special focus of mind to a godly parent to lay before the dear young people the sobering realities of eternity, death, and judgment to come. "Tell it to the generation following." What a beautiful sight to see the little ones in the house of prayer, and a godly parent should make attendance at church a law of the house. It is recorded of Abraham, "He will command his children, and his household after him."

I feel a godly father or mother needs constant grace to exercise being firm to enforce what is right. Severity and firmness are two distinct words. A command may be enforced with a firm contention for its fulfillment without severity or harsh methods. What is firmness? "Let your yea be yea, and your nay be nay, lest ye fall into condemnation." Such a training of youth will lead a parent into the pleasant promise, "Her children rise up and call her blessed."

I have dropped these "ears" of friendly counsel for parents who profess to know the truth, and who feel the burden of parental responsibility. Some parent may say "Alas, I wish I could train my children in the right way; I would seek their best welfare, but I come so far short of what a parent should be." The Word of God shows us one sure way of training a child in the way he should go – "Let us therefore come boldly unto the throne of grace, that we may obtain mercy, and find grace to help in time of need." The secret lies in the word "grace." The Lord will give grace to the needy; He will give wisdom to those who ask it. He will give help to us to be a daily example to those who live near us; grace, to be living sermons to the young. And so, godly, anxious-hearted fathers and mothers, "Grace be with you."

Warnings by the Wayside

"Ponder the path of thy feet" – Proverbs 4:26

My dear young friends, it is my heartfelt prayer that the blessing of the Lord be upon you. What do I mean by "the blessing of the Lord"? I mean, a knowledge of God's truth that will save you. As I write these pages, my heart is filled with the solemn thought, "Every boy and girl reading these pages is hastening to an eternal destination – heaven or hell!" O that the God of truth might be pleased to write the word "eternity" into your consciences! Every rising sun – every night we go to our beds – eternity is drawing nearer and nearer to us. And who can tell how soon we may enter into eternity?

"Only this frail and fleeting breath
Preserves me from the jaws of death;
Soon as it fails, at once I'm gone,
And plunged into a world unknown."

So now, my dear young friend, it is my earnest desire that the Holy Spirit might help me write to you. I will share with you words of truth, in great simplicity. The foundation of what I hope to say to you is the word of advice which Solomon gave in the days in which he lived: "Ponder the path of thy feet," Proverbs 4:26. The word "ponder" means "consider, think upon, weigh well." The pathway of life is beset with many snares and pitfalls and traps for the young. We sing,

91

"Childhood's years are passing o'er us,
Youthful days will soon be gone;
Cares and sorrows lie before us,
Hidden dangers, snares unknown."

One of the great objects of Sunday Schools is to show you the dangers and pitfalls in the pathway of life. The Word of God is full of solemn warnings, which your teachers try to set before you. I want to call your attention to some of these warnings.

I have often learned a lesson when journeying about the country, from the bill-boards which are set up along the way. I have no doubt that all of you have seen such notices as these: "dangerous corner"; "trespassers will be prosecuted"; "beware of the dog", and many such cautions to the passers-by. May I help you glean some helpful advice and reminders of moral teachings from these? For they illustrate some of the good counsel contained in the Word of God.

WATCH YOUR STEP!

How often we meet with this caution, and how needful it is that we "watch the step", when a fall may mean injury, even broken bones. If we are to watch the step that leads us into the public building, or the step which leads us into the store, all the more, watch the step that leads you into bad company.

My dear young friends, mind the <u>first</u> step and you shall not be exposed to many dangers from the later ones. For instance, the first lie you tell; this is a first act of deceit which is but a first step in what proves to many to be their Road to Ruin. I say, Watch Your Step!

If you could visit the gloomy cells of the prisons in our land, and talk with those miserable prisoners, you would find that many of them *now* know it was because they neglected the warning to Watch Your Step that they took the road that leads to a prison cell. If you would have mercy following you, my dear young friends, then do remember the solemn fact, "Thou, God, seest me." For, "the eyes of the Lord are in every place, beholding the evil and the good."

I lately read an incident in which a little boy proved the verse, "Be sure your sin will find you out." A good man was paying a visit to a friend by the sea-side, and upon entering the dining-room, he saw a photograph of a little boy in the act of stealing.

The little boy was the son of the master of the house. He had climbed up the second shelf of the cupboard, and was holding on to the shelf with one hand, and with the other clasping a pot of jam, and was about to enjoy a stolen feast. At this point the boy's father, who was an amateur photographer, came in carrying his camera. He saw his little boy at the cupboard, and he soon had a snapshot. A framed enlargement was hung up for the little fellow to be reminded of his breach of the command, "Thou shalt not steal." This little boy would have preserved himself from such an act if he had heeded the warning, Watch Your Step!

Watch Your Step when tempted by ungodly companions to break the Sabbath day. The Word of God is very plain, "Remember the Sabbath day, to keep it holy." It is such a sad sight to see so many millions bent on pleasure, on the day which belongs to the Lord. Do we not see a tragic sign of the last days in this breaking of the Sabbath: "In the last days, men shall be lovers of pleasure more than lovers of God." Boys and girls, "ponder the path of your feet," and watch those steps that lead you to disregard the house of prayer and break the command, "Remember the Sabbath."

One step which often leads to sad consequences is Disobedience to Parents. I feel sorry when I see boys and girls who do not willingly do the tasks which father or mother have set them to; and boys and girls who do not show the respect which is due their parents, but answer them back rudely when they wish them to do little duties and errands. My dear young friends, Watch Your Step. "Honour thy father and thy mother."

I earnestly hope you may be enabled to pay attention to the warning, Watch Your Step, as I tell you about a little servant maid who took a step on the downward road and then was led later to confess her folly in doing wrong. This little girl had finished her school years and entered upon a situation as a servant to a mistress who was very kind to her. She soon gained a good reputation and earned the praises of her mistress for her dutiful behaviour, and all went well until one day she was washing up a valuable tea-set, and broke some cups and saucers in so doing. What did the little servant do? She feared that her mistress would be angry with her, and instead of telling her the truth, she began to think what she could do to hide the broken china.

At last she thought of a plan, and she went out into the garden, and buried the broken cups and saucers out of sight. Thus took she the first step of deception and dishonesty. She went to bed, but she could not sleep, and the next day when she was going about her daily duties, she carried a guilty conscience and could not look her mistress in the face. On the second evening she tried to rest, and again a guilty conscience would not allow her to sleep, and at length she resolved to tell her mistress and beg her forgiveness. She arose from her bed, and went to the room of her mistress, and knocked at the door, and confessed her act of deception in seeking to cover up her carelessness in washing up the tea-set. Her mistress listened to her sad tale, and then said "I would rather have all my costly china broken to pieces than to have a servant maid who would deceive me, and be afraid to tell me the truth." Forgiveness was granted, and the girl went back to her room, and having now dispensed with her guilty conscience, she soon fell happily asleep. I would like to have told that little servant maid that, while her mistress could only forgive her for breaking her china, and lying to her, that the precious blood of Jesus Christ could do more – yes, could wash away the sin which had brought her that guilty conscience!

So, speak the truth, dear boys and girls, and when tempted to do what is contrary to the Word of God, Watch Your Step.

"God is in heaven! Can He see
When I am doing wrong?
Yes, that He can; He looks at me
All day and all night long."

KEEP THE GATE SHUT!

Another notice-board which teaches a useful lesson is this caution: Keep the Gate Shut. This is often seen in town and country, is it not? How much trouble is prevented in life if only the gates are kept shut!

I shall mention three gates which all boys and girls will find make such a warning needful and wise. They are:

1st, Eye-Gate.
2nd, Ear-Gate.
3rd, Lip-Gate.

1st, Keep the *Eye-Gate* Shut!

The Bible has many stories in which sin against God entered in at Eye-Gate. If that man called Achan, who lived in Old Testament days, had kept Eye-Gate shut, he would not have fallen into the snare of deceit and robbery. He is told of in the Book of Joshua, chapters 6 and 7. O what a sad record he makes of the fact, "Be sure your sin will find you out!" The Word of God tells us the command went forth that the children of Israel were not to take any of the spoils of battle when the city of Jericho was taken, and the treasures of silver and gold, and the vessels of brass and iron were to be consecrated to the Lord. But Achan, when he saw the good things of the city, disobeyed the commands and took some items that he coveted to possess, and hid them in his tent. Then it was that the next time the children of Israel went out to battle at Ai, they were defeated, and the Lord showed Joshua, who led the people, that His command had been broken. The Lord commanded Joshua that he was to go through the camps of Israel and examine the people, one by one, until he found the guilty person.

What thoughts must have passed through Achan's mind while the search was conducted! He waited his turn to be examined, with a guilty conscience, and when he stood before Joshua at last, how he must have trembled at the thoughts of his sin. The Word of God tells us, "And Joshua said unto Achan, 'Tell me now what thou hast done.' And Achan answered Joshua, and said, 'When I *saw* among the spoils a goodly Babylonish garment, and two hundred shekels of silver, and a wedge of gold, of fifty shekels weight, then I coveted them, and took them; and behold, they are hid in the earth in the midst of my tent, and the silver under it." What a solemn confession, my dear young friends! The judgment of the Lord was meted out to Achan and his household also. Everything belonging to the poor man was gathered together in the sight of all the people, and then the Word of God tells us, "And all Israel stoned him with stones, and burned them with fire, after they had stoned them. And they raised over him a great heap of stones." The tomb of Achan was a powerful sermon on the text, "Be not deceived; God is not mocked; whatsoever a man soweth, that shall he also reap."

Remember the warning, "Keep the Gate Shut." A good Puritan man named John Flavel used to pray,

"*O, may my eye kept closed to be*
To what concerns me not to see."

A look may lead to covetous desires; covetous desires may lead to wrong actions; wrong actions may lead to the loss of character, position, and a good name.

2nd, Keep the *Ear-Gate* Shut!

As you go about the world, boys and girls, you will often hear conversation which can do you no good at all – idle talk, foolish jesting, tales, the oath of the wicked. Remember the warning "Keep the Gate Shut," when in such company. No tongue can tell the mischief which enters into youthful minds by way of Ear-Gate. Do not lend your ears to any boys or girls who seek to entice you into paths of evil. "My son, if sinners entice thee, consent thou not." Abstain from evil companions. Many a young life has been ruined when the first step towards it has been mixing with bad companions and allowing their evil counsel to enter in at Ear-Gate.

A father taught his boy a useful lesson on the danger of evil company. The boy was given to going about with other boys who did not walk in straight paths, and his father, wishing to break him of the habit, one day brought him home a basket of apples. He gave them to his son, who was very pleased with the present. Upon examination, the boy found one of the apples was rotten. He took it out, and his father observing him, said, "George, why take that one out?"

"Oh," said George, "It will make all the rest bad."

"Well," said his father, "is it not possible the good apples will make the rotten one good, like themselves?"

"Of course not," answered George.

Then his father used the illustration to good purpose, and pointed out how evil companions corrupt good morals. It was a lesson the lad never forgot. Boys and girls, remember the dangers of letting in evil conversation and naughty suggestions at Ear-Gate. "Keep the Gate Shut!"

3rd, Keep the *Lip-Gate* Shut!

O, what angry words sometimes pass through this gate! "The tongue is a fire," James 3:6. A lighted match carelessly dropped by the passer-by will burn down a farmer's entire haystack. An idle word, a word spoken without thought, an angry word, O what sad havoc one wrong word can do among loved ones and friends!

> *"For many a shaft at random sent*
> *Finds mark the archer never meant;*
> *And many a word at random spoken,*
> *May wound, or soothe a heart that's broken."*

An old writer said, "It is better to be a bee that gathers the honey than a wasp which stings."

> *"Angry words are lightly spoken,*
> *In a rash and thoughtless hour;*
> *Brightest links of life are broken*
> *By their deep, insidious power.*
>
> *Hearts inspired by warmest feeling,*
> *Ne'er before by anger stirred,*
> *Oft are rent past human feeling*
> *By a single angry word."*

It would be a great mercy, my dear young friends, if the Lord should be pleased to put the prayer of a godly man within you: "Set a watch, O Lord, before my mouth; keep the door of my lips."

People carelessly say, "Have you heard the news about So-and-So?" and they pass on some tale. But the Word of God denounces tale-bearing. "Thou shalt not go up and down as a talebearer among thy people," and "Where no wood is, there the fire goeth out; and where there is no talebearer, there the strife ceaseth." It would be wise if young and old always weighed the words of their lips in the scales of truth.

" Words give pleasure, words give pain,
Words are wise, and words are vain;
Words are false, and words are true,
Words weigh most when they are few."

"In a mixed conversation," says John Newton, "it is a good rule to say nothing, without a just cause, to the disadvantage of others. I was once in a large company of persons, where some severe things were spoken of a certain Mr. Wilson, when one person wisely observed that he had never known any evil man to be converted or convinced of his sins, by what was said of him behind his back."

May I suggest that every statement which you permit to pass through Lip-Gate be tested by three questions:

1st, **Is it True?**
2nd, **Is it Kind?**
3rd, **Is it Necessary?**

Wrong words and unkind remarks are the like the Australian boomerang, which returns to the person who throws it; and so boys and girls, remember the solemn warning, "For every idle word that men shall speak, they shall give account thereof in the day of judgment." So, Keep the Lip-Gate Shut!

THIS
WATER
NOT
FIT FOR
DRINKING!

The next notice is a wise and kindly warning: "This Water Not Fit For Drinking," seen by some wayside pools and ponds. But there would be another place it would do us all good for this notice to be found. For, I sometimes look in bookshop windows, and as I examine the contents of the shelves, I feel it could be said of thousands of those books, "This Water Not Fit For Drinking." Do you understand my meaning?

"These books are not fit for people to read," it may as well say. The bottles in the chemist's shop are often marked with a red label, "Poison," and many gaily covered books are full of erroneous teaching, and could be truly labeled "Poison." Boys and girls, beware of bad books! One hymnwriter sings:

"All worthless books away I'd throw
Whatever may result;
These eyes were never given, I know,
My Maker to insult!

"Lord, give me grace to shun all books
Which lead from heaven and Thee;
And make Thy Word, Most Holy One,
More precious unto me."

A huge bonfire could be made if all the books which ought not to be on the bookshelves of people who profess the truth were gathered together in an heap. Fathers and mothers, be careful what books you put into the hands of your little ones!

I have read of a little lad who was fond of bad books, and was found at the bottom of the class because he read such books instead of learning useful lessons which would fit him for the duties of every-day life.

"Tom," said his father one day, "carry that pitcher down to the well."

"I must empty it first," answered Tom, "for it is full of mud."

"Never mind, Tom," replied his father, "just carry it down to the well."

"But it's no use," said Tom; "see, father, it is quite filled with the mud."

"Take the pitcher," he answered, "just as it is, and dip it into the well."

Tom carried his burden to the well, and brought it back only a little heavier, and as full of mud as before.

"My boy," then said his father, "when you try to learn your lessons at school with a head filled with silly tales which you have read, think of this pitcher of mud you tried to fill at the well."

My dear young friends, when you pick up a book of the style of most novels today, or any other book which is contrary to the Word of God, think of the sign warning you: "This Water Not Fit For Drinking!"

Good John Newton said, "I have many books that I cannot sit down and read; I have some silver books, and a very few golden books. But I have one book worth them all: the Bible."

DANGEROUS CORNER!

Another notice one frequently sees along the roadsides is the warning, Dangerous Corner. The pathway of life contains many dangerous corners, and boys and girls, I do most affectionately warn you to "ponder the path of thy feet."

One "dangerous corner" occurs in life when a young person first concludes his school and goes out into the busy world to earn "the bread which perisheth." O how many youths and maidens begin right then to depart from honest ways and lose their integrity. I would counsel you to do what is right and "abstain from all appearance of evil." Do not enter into any situation, or occupation, in which you are required to break the Sabbath day, and do what is wrong. Beware of such a "Dangerous Corner." And remember the blessing and privilege of being able to hear the gospel preached in its purity, and enter not into any path of labour which will prevent you attending the house of prayer.

Another dangerous corner is when boys and girls become young men and women, and begin to form friendships which may lead to a united journey through life. O this is an important step! "Ponder the path of thy feet" in such a solemn matter, and remember in turning this dangerous corner, that "How can two walk together, except they be agreed?"

I have tried to lay some moral truths before you and to give you helpful advice and instruction. I wish you well in your journey through life, and I earnestly hope you may grow up useful and honourable men and women.

THIS BRIDGE IS NOT SAFE

When I was walking one day in a country lane, I came upon a canal bridge where this important caution was posted, and I would have crossed it, had it not been for the sign! This is a warning which can remind us of matters of unspeakable importance. Fixed on a notice-board was the sign, This Bridge Is Not Safe! May to use this to affectionately warn you of the vital distinction between *morality* and *real religion?*

It is good, my dear young friends, to be upright in your dealings, and truthful, and honest; it is good to go to Sunday School and the house of prayer, and be obedient and dutiful children; but, if you hope to go to heaven by doing these things, I warn you, This Bridge Is Not Safe.

The only *safe* bridge is the finished work of Jesus Christ. It is His doing and His dying that saves us, or we are not saved. His precious blood and His spotless righteousness; on this bridge you find a sure foundation, and every redeemed soul that travels over this bridge safely crosses the river of death into the realms of everlasting bliss. No man ever entered the gates of glory by good works. "By grace are ye saved, through faith, and that not of yourselves, it is the gift of God; not of works, lest any man should boast." I know it is the anxious, prayerful desire of those who seek your best welfare that the Holy Spirit might be pleased to begin the good work of grace in you. The God of truth, Who gave us the Word of God, is the author of all real religion. O may this solemn fact be deeply engraved in your hearts.

It will rejoice the hearts of those who love you to watch you grow up into useful, truthful and honest men and women; and if the Lord should open your hearts and eyes, like He did Lydia of old (Acts 16), and lay you low at the feet of Jesus as guilty, needy, repentant sinners. O, what an unspeakable mercy for you, my dear young friends! O may the God of truth bestow this invaluable blessing upon you!

" ' *Tis true religion which can give*
The sweetest pleasures while we live;
'Tis true religion must supply
The solid comfort when we die."

The Four T's

There are four "T"s too apt to run,
'Tis best to set a watch upon.

O watch your *Thoughts,* they ramble oft,
They run aground, they soar aloft.
Oft when alone they take them wings,
And light upon forbidden things.

Your *Temter* watch, if one you have,
Think well, speak slow, if strife you'd save;
An angry word, a temper lost,
No tongue can tell how great the cost.

O watch your *Tongue,* for many tell
Of slips they've had – O learn it well;
Know when to speak, and be content
When silence is most eloquent.

O watch your *Time,* my little maid,
Life with its years will soon have fled;
Yea, like the sand runs through the glass,
The moments fly – "All flesh is grass."

If ye who read would watch each "T",
The God of *Truth* will strengthen thee.

Broken Hedges

"whose breaketh an hedge, a serpent shall bite him." – Ecclesiastes 10:8

A hedge is a familiar sight to every boy and girl. The farmer protects his field, and the roads are bounded, with an hedge, which provides a barrier and a protection at the same time. I want to talk to you, my dear young readers, about "moral hedges." The Word of God sets up many hedges of wise caution and instruction, designed to keep us all in paths of morality and integrity. It is my privilege to instruct you in the needs-be of these hedges, to preserve you from the dangers that will beset you in everyday life. When people break through these hedges because they feel there is something they want, it results in their great sorrow.

The first I shall mention is **The Hedge of Obedience.** One of the signs of the last times, the Apostle Paul wrote, is "disobedience to parents", 2 Timothy 3:2, and surely such a sign can be observed in many homes up and down the land.

The dictionary says, "Obedient – doing as one is told." Alas, such boys and girls are becoming rare. I have noticed how some boys and girls behave when mother says, "I want you to go to the shop for me," or, "I want you to chop up some firewood," and many like commands. O the unwillingness of some boys and girls to wait upon a good mother, or run errands, and perform little tasks to help in the duties of home life! Can a disobedient boy or girl grow up into a dependable, trustworthy man or woman? The faithful warnings and admonition of parents are the outcome of parental love. And when father or mother say, "Do not do this!" and "Do not do that!" they design your good and profit in days to come.

Disobedience has proved to be the entry-gate to many a prison door and a stepping-stone to the poorhouse. "Children, obey your parents." The days will quickly come when your fathers and mothers will be gone. Do not grieve them by disobedient acts and unkind words.

I will tell you how a father taught his little son a useful lesson. He was a forgetful boy, and disobedient also, so his father made him drive a nail into a door whenever he was found out in a wrong act. Bye and bye, the door was covered with nails, and the little boy felt ashamed to look at it.

When his father saw the door was filled with nails, he said, "My son, I will tell you what I will do. Every time you quickly obey father or mother in what we tell you to do, and when you do a kind action, I will take a nail out." The boy said "I will try, father." Day after day went by, and the nails went from the door one by one, and the day came when the last nail was pulled out. The boy watched his father pull out the nail, and then said, "O father, all the marks are still left!"

Yes, my dear young friends, disobedience to parents or teachers, and wrong-doing, will leave sad marks in the mind, and lead to painful reflections when you grow up. O think of the consequences of breaking through the Hedge of Obedience! "Be sure your sin will find you out." "Whoso breaketh an hedge, a serpent shall bite him."

Now, we should speak of **The Hedge of Punctuality.** I am sure if an invitation came for you to visit King George V. at Buckingham Palace you would be sure to get there in time. How careful you would be to have clean hands and face, and well-polished boots! And yet boys and girls come late to church and ignore punctuality. Do you know that the house of prayer is the visiting place of the King of kings? O what disrespect it would show to be late when visiting King George V. at an appointed time? And how much greater the lack of respect to the truth, and the God of truth, in coming late to chapel.

A soldier engaged in warfare against the enemies of his country was taken captive and cast into prison. Being a blacksmith in private life, he examined the chain which held him fast, and found by the marks upon it that it was one of his own making, and so knew that it would never permit his escape. And bad habits of being late are like the links of a chain which becomes stronger and stronger until unbreakable by human effort. Lazy boys and girls become lazy men and women, and find themselves bound by chains which they forged in the days of youth. If boys and girls are not in time for school, they will not be in time in later days when filling various occupations in life.

As important as any hedge is, **The Hedge of Honesty.** A hedge is broken little by little. At first, a mere twig or two is moved, and then a larger hole is made. Bye and bye, the boy can creep through to rob the farmer's orchard. And boys and girls begin to tread the path of dishonesty little by little. A stolen apple, a penny, some marbles, a little thing, and thus the Hedge of Honesty is broken through. Beware of dishonesty in little things.

I will tell you a true incident which will shew the damage a little thing can do. An overseer in a calico mill found a pin lodged in a machine which cost the firm about three hundred dollars; an ordinary pin, such as you buy in a farthing packet.

Calicoes, after they are printed and washed, are dried and smoothed by being passed over heated rollers. Well, by some mischance, a pin dropped so as to lie upon the principal roller, and indeed, became wedged into it, the head standing out a little way from the surface.

Over and over went the roller, and round and round went the cloth, winding at length upon another roller, until the piece was finished off. Then another piece began to be dried and wound; and so on, until a hundred pieces had been counted off. When at length they came to be inspected, it was found that there were holes in every piece throughout the web, and only three-quarters of a yard apart!

Of course, these items could not be classified as in good condition; so they were sold as remnants at less than half the price they would have brought, had it not been for that hidden pin. Only a pin!

Dishonest habits are often formed by boys and girls mixing in bad company. If you pick up a lump of coal you will have black fingers, and boys and girls will obtain a blackened character in bad company. "My son, if sinners entice thee, consent thou not!" (Proverbs 1:10)

Godly Mr. Tiptaft once gave an address to boys and girls – a short one. Upon being asked to speak, he stood up and said: "Beware of bad company!" Then he raised his voice and repeated, "Beware of bad company!" A third time, he raised his voice to a louder key, and called out, "Beware of bad company!" There he ended his address. Do you think that those boys and girls ever forgot the voice of that godly minister, ringing out those words of warning?

Beware of breaking through the Hedge of Honesty. "Thou God seest me" (Gen. 16:13). Ananias and Sapphira broke through the hedge, and O, how dearly they paid! The principle of honesty is a stepping-stone to honourable and useful occupations in life. Have you never seen the notice hung: "An honest boy wanted"? Yes, and thousands of honest boys and girls wanted to grow up into honest men and women, and become a strength to the land we love.

How vital to our land is **The Hedge of Industry.** What a complaint is laziness! If we had hospitals in our land where lazy people could be treated, I fear they would be filled every day! – with lazy fellows who dislike honest toil.

"Some think it an hardship to work for their bread,
Although for our good it was meant;

*But those who won't work have no right to be fed,
And the idle are never content."*

The busy bee which hastens from flower to flower to gather winter's store, and the little ant which toils all the summer long for the same purpose, both rebuke lazy folks. "Go to the ant, thou sluggard, consider her ways, and be wise; which having no guide, overseer, or ruler, provideth her meat in the summer, and gathereth her food in the harvest." (Proverbs 6:6-8)

It is a pleasant sight to see busy boys and girls occupied with the little duties of home life. Little tasks, well-done, lay the foundation for an industrious career through life. I remember a song of my schooldays:

*"If I were a cobbler, I'd make it my pride
The best of all cobblers to be;
If I were a tinker, no tinker beside,
Should mend an old kettle like me."*

Begin at the bottom of the ladder, my dear young friends, and climb up, rung by rung, by honest service. The acorn grows into the giant oak, and many an humble apprentice lad has obtained a good name in business life. "Be content with such things as ye have," and do not waste the valuable days of life with coveting the things of others.

I have thought much of a statement in the Word of God concerning working folk of ancient days, when the prophet Haggai told the children of Israel, "he that earneth wages, earneth wages to put into a bag with holes." (Haggai 1:6) And when youths and maidens spend their money at the picture-palace, or in the public house, or on bad books, or gambling, and other so-called pleasures of earth, what is such foolish conduct but putting wages into a "bag with holes"?

The prison and the poor-house lie on the other side of the Hedge of Industry.

How can we live without **The Hedge of Kindness?** A kind action, a kind word, is like oil upon squeaking wheels. My dear young friends, I would affectionately warn you to be kind to your father and mother. Many boys and girls wound their parents by disobedient acts, naughty words, bad tempers, and in many ways. Be kind to your brothers and sisters; it is a pleasant sight to see a united family. Be kind even to helpless animals. O what a sad sight to see a boy or girl ill-treat one of God's creatures!

"How should I like it, if I were a fly,
To have my wings torn by boys passing by?
How should I like it, if I were a cat,
To have my tail pulled, and all such as that?

How should I like it, if I were a dog,
A donkey, a horse, a beetle, or frog,
If boys should seek fun in giving me pain?
I never should like it; I say then again,
Let this be my question, a wise one, I see,
How should I like it, if done unto me?"

And I would drop a special word of caution: boys and girls, be kind to the aged, the infirm, and the crippled. Never, never ridicule poor afflicted folk. Who gave you health and strength? Who gave you eyes and ears, hands and tongue and feet? Who gave you the wonderfully made body in which you dwell?

I will relate to you the sad confession of a boy which I gleaned from an old book – a true incident:

A boy was playing with his schoolfellows one day, when a stage-coach drove up, and a number of passengers alighted. Among the number was an elderly man with a stick, who got out with much difficulty, and when he had stepped out onto the ground, he walked in a most curious way. His feet turned one way and his knees another. The boy shouted out, with no thought, "Look at old Rattlebones!" and the other boys took up the cry. The poor man turned his head with a look of pain and then just went on his way.

Just then the father of the boy came round the corner, and shook hands heartily with the man, and assisted him to his own house, which was but a little distance. The boy looked on with a guilty conscience, and he could not anymore enjoy his play.

At tea-time he went home, and soon he was required to enter the sitting-room, to be introduced to this poor, afflicted stranger. He went there with trembling! It so happened the man did not recognize him as the lad who had mocked him so recently, and said to the father, "Such a fine boy he is; he was surely worth saving."

These words cut the boy to the heart. His father had often told him of a kind friend who had plunged into the river to save him from drowning, while he was an infant, and who, as a consequence, had been made a cripple by rheumatism; and so it turned out that this was the very man he had made a laughing-stock, by calling him "old Rattlebones." Such a lesson was stamped upon the boy's mind, from that day, that he ever after sought to be kind to the afflicted.

The Hedge of Kindness is sometimes broken through, when boys and girls give way to uncontrolled tempers, and unkind words and acts follow.

"Be not swift to take offense,
Let it pass!

Anger is a foe to sense,
Let it pass!

Brood not darkly o'er a wrong,
Which will disappear ere long,
Let it pass!

Nothing is more important than **The Hedge of Truth.** A merchant, one day, received a valuable order for a large quantity of goods. The next day another letter came canceling the order, but the merchant handed the note to his clerk, saying, "I want you to answer this note. Please say that the goods were shipped before the letter recalling the order was received."

"I'm very sorry, Sir, but I can't do it," replied the clerk with much humility.

"You can't do it! And pray boy, why not?" asked the merchant angrily.

"Because, Sir, the goods are in the yard now, and it would be telling a lie."

What did the merchant do? Did he dismiss the clerk who spoke the truth? Oh no! He knew the value of such an employee, and so he made the boy his confidential clerk, and entrusted his business arrangements into his safe hands. Employers want boys and girls who speak the truth!

O, what sad consequences come from lying and deceit! May I tell you of another?

A blind woman who lived with her daughter one day lost a silver spoon, and she asked her daughter if she had seen it. The daughter said "No, mother, I have not!" But some time after the question was presented again to her by her mother, "Have you taken my spoon?" The girl, in a rage, dared the Almighty to strike her dead if she had the spoon in her possession. She immediately fell down, and when the neighbours came in, the lost spoon was found hidden in her dress. Dare you think this a silly story? Or, boys and girls, in the Word of God is there a solemn reality that "whoever loves a lie" can never enter the gates of heaven?

"Be the outcome what it may,
Always speak the truth;
Whether work or whether play,
Always speak the truth.

Never from this rule depart,
Grave it deeply on your heart.
Written 'tis in Virtue's chart;
Always speak the truth."

May I speak to you of one more "hedge"?

You must learn to hear **The Hedge of Conscience.** My young friends, always, always listen to this voice, with the utmost of attention. Have you not noticed a "something" within you, which checks you and rebukes you when you wish to do wrong? A voice which whispers in your soul, "You are doing wrong! You are doing wrong!" This is the voice of conscience, a warning monitor. Every boy and girl is the subject of a natural conscience, which accuses and condemns when you do wrong, or when you tell lies, or when you do not behave with kindness.

A conscience is like the reins which drive a horse: the driver guides and checks with a pull. And when a person wanders into paths of sin, conscience gives a pull to warn and caution. Alas, how many boys and girls pay no heed to the warnings of conscience, but go on and on in wrong-doing, and later fall into disgrace. O, beware of breaking through the hedge of conscience!

I have read of a poor Indian who was feeling the pangs of conscience. One day he asked a white man if he might have some tobacco, who gave him a handful from his pocket. The day following, the Indian came back, enquiring for the donor, saying that he had found a coin among the tobacco. But other men said "You may as well keep it! It was his mistake and not yours." But the Indian man answered, pointing to his heart: "I got a good man and a bad man here; and the good man say, 'It is not mine, so I must return it to the owner;' the bad man say 'Why? He gave it to you and it is your own now.' The good man say, 'That not right, the tobacco is yours, not the money;' the bad man say 'Never mind, you got it, go and buy something.' The good man say, "No, no! You must not do so.' So I don't know what to do, and I think I go to sleep; but the good man and the bad man keep talking all night and trouble me; and now I bring the money back I feel glad." And does not this Indian man put many of us to shame? The pathway of honesty is bounded by the Hedge of Conscience.

You will remember my text: "Whoso breaketh an hedge, a serpent shall bite him." I have tried to set before you some moral truths which serve as "hedges" to keep boys and girls in right paths.

But now – we have talked about breaking through the hedge, but I wish to move on to tell you about the serpent's bite. For, our text says of the hedge-breaker, "a serpent shall bite him." The serpent's bite is a solemn emblem of sin and its consequences. If a man is bitten by a serpent, no tongue can tell the agony and pain which wracks his body from head to foot. Sight fails, and the hearing departs; the tongue cleaves to the roof of the mouth, and the hand drops useless; the feet refuse to move, and madness makes the serpent-bitten man a pitiable object. Only death, which soon comes, can end the pain; no earthly physician can eradicate the serpent's venom from the blood, and no remedy can bring about a cure. And the serpent-bitten man is a picture of a sinner dead in sin.

My dear young friends, I would try to shew you the sad state in which every boy and girl comes into the world.

The Word of God says, "born in sin." All boys and girls enter the world already suffering from the consequences of the serpent bite of sin, the venom of which runs in every vein. "All have sinned." And what is the result? All persons are ruined and undone sinners. O may the God of truth help me to set before you two solemn and important facts:

1ˢᵗ, The Awful Malady of Sin
2ⁿᵈ, The Only Remedy for Sin

1ˢᵗ, **The Awful Malady of Sin** which is described by the serpent's bite. You hear pastors in the pulpit of your church talk of the ruin of Adam's fall. What do they mean by "Adam's fall?" The Word of God contains a sad story of how Adam and Eve broke through an hedge set up by God, and as a consequence, became prey to the serpent bite of sin, and brought ruin to all mankind. See Genesis chapter three.

Adam and Eve were placed in the Garden of Eden by the good Lord. They were surrounded by beauties and pleasures untold; no tongue can tell what a wonderful place the Garden of Eden must have been. A solemn command was given by the Lord, "Of every tree in the garden thou mayest freely eat; but of the tree of the knowledge of good and evil, thou shalt not eat of it: for in the day that thou eatest thereof thou shalt surely die" (Genesis 2:16-17).

I have no doubt Adam and Eve lived very happily for a time, but alas! Quite soon the command was disobeyed. The Word of God tells how a cunning serpent crept into the beautiful garden and began to talk to Eve. "How could a serpent talk?" say you. O, have I not told you yet? It was the devil in the form of a serpent. This so-called "serpent" then said to Eve, "Yea, hath God said, 'Ye shall not eat of every tree of the garden?'" And he went on to instill poisonous thoughts and inclinations into the mind of Eve, and bye and bye, she broke through the hedge. "And when the woman saw that the tree was good for food, and that it was pleasant to the eyes, and a tree to be desired to make one wise, she took of the fruit thereof, and did eat; and gave also unto her husband with her; and he did eat" (Genesis 3:6). O the sad consequences which followed!

Soon the Lord entered the garden and found Adam and Eve ashamed, and afraid, and unable to meet His holy eyes. O how solemn it must have been when Adam and Eve were arraigned, like the guilty prisoners they were, before the bar of an offended God! The Lord visited their sin upon them with lasting consequences. The ground was cursed and permitted to bring forth thorns and thistles; and Adam was sentenced to till the ground, and earn his bread by the sweat of his brow. Eve was solemnly punished also.

But worst of all – ah, far worse – is, added to all these sad effects of sin, the enforcement of God's law: "In the day that thou eatest thereof, thou shalt surely die." Yes, the beginnings of pain and affliction and death entered into the bodies of Adam and Eve, and they became dying creatures; and every boy and girl from that day to this comes into this world a fallen sinner. "Sin entered into the world, and death by sin." (Romans 5:12)

And the saddest part of breaking through the hedge was that Adam and Eve were turned out of the presence of God, and no more allowed to dwell in the Garden of Eden. O what an awful breach was made by sin! No brush can paint the sad picture of a ruined world; the effects of the serpent bite of sin are seen on every hand. The hymn-writer sings:

"O thou hideous monster sin,
What a curse hast thou brought in!
All creation groans through thee,
Growing cause of misery."

The poor people groaning on hospital beds, and the sad inmates of the asylums, set forth the dire effects of Adam's fall. War, with all of its horrors, and the misery and degradation in the slums of the city all teach the same truth: look how much harm sin hath wrought!

But the most grievous effects of the serpent bite are seen in fallen man's actions and deeds. For we read of sinners in the Word of God, that we are "dead in trespasses and sins." What does this mean? It sets forth what is your true nature now. Like the serpent bite, which causes a loss of every sense and feeling, so sin entered the heart of Adam and Eve, and through them has entered the heart of everyone who ever lived, or who ever will live, even you.

Adam's fall has sunk poor sinners so low that no boy or girl can think a good thought, or speak a good word, or do a good action, or take one step in the narrow way which leads to eternal life, unless God enables you. By the word "good" you see that I mean "spiritual" and "holy." Sin has filled the heart with a deadly poison which causes every boy and girl to love by nature what is wrong, and hate by nature what is heavenly and spiritual and righteous.

The sad effect of the serpent's bite is eternal! Yes, that bite has not only brought death and misery and the grave, but a never-ending eternity of woe to every sinner who dies without a God-given repentance, and heartfelt knowledge of the truth. Such is the malady of sin, my dear young readers; sin has brought chaos and confusion into the earth, and ruin and misery to guilty men.

But this all makes me happy to set before you, 2ndly:

2nd, The Only Remedy For Sin. This wonderful fact is true! There is a remedy for sin, for this serpent's bite.

If we go north, south, east, and west to find an earthly physician to cure a poor man bitten by this serpent, we shall search in vain; for there is no remedy beneath the sun to heal the serpent bite of sin. This world has no healing medicine for the sin-bitten. The remedy for sin comes from heaven, and is revealed to man by the Word of God.

A beautiful picture of the serpent bite of sin and its cure was set forth in the days of old when the children of Israel wandered in the wilderness. These people were not content; they broke through the Hedge of Contentment, and they grumbled at the food God gave them. So the Bible says, "The Lord sent fiery serpents among the people, and they bit the people: and much people of Israel died" (Numbers 21:6). Yes, too late the children of Israel saw the evil of breaking hedges, and they went to Moses and admitted their guilt, and begged him to intercede on their behalf. "And Moses prayed for the people" (Numbers 21:7).

So merciful is God that He gave Moses this command: "Make thee a fiery serpent, and set it on a pole: and it shall come to pass, that every one that is bitten, when he looketh upon it shall live. And Moses made a serpent of brass, and put it upon a pole, and it came to pass that if a serpent had bitten any man, when he beheld the serpent of brass, he lived" (Numbers 21:8-9). What a wonderful cure! And what a wonderful picture of the cure of the serpent sin! The Word of God tells us, "And as Moses lifted up the serpent in the wilderness, even so must the Son of Man be lifted up: that whosoever believeth in Him should not perish, but have eternal life." (John 3:14-15).

This is the only remedy for the sin-bitten, my dear young friends! None but Jesus can do helpless sinners good. O what a mercy, if the Holy Spirit should convince you of your lost estate as sinners and shew you the way of salvation.

When George Whitefield was preaching up and down our country, a gentleman who heard him was filled with great distress of mind. He felt his sins to be so great a burden, he could not eat, he could not sleep, and he could not attend to his business.

One evening the Countess of Huntingdon, a godly woman of the 18th century, who was in company where he was present, heard him say to a friend, "I am a lost man! My sins are too great to be forgiven; I cannot be saved."

118

"I am glad to hear it," said the Countess.

"What?! Can it be possible you feel glad that I am lost forever?" said he.

"I repeat it, yes," she replied. "I am heartily glad of it; because the Scripture says, 'The Son of Man is come to seek and to save that which was lost.'"

The gentleman burst into tears and exclaimed, "Oh, how precious those words are!"

What does this teach us? It teaches us that the first step toward a remedy for the serpent bite of sin is feeling your sense of need, a felt knowledge of the deadly disease, what is called "conviction of sin." The Holy Spirit accomplishes this wonderful work in pricking the heart to feel the malady and guilt of sin, and opening the eyes to see the solemn consequences of it. The sinner is made to know the tremendous truth, "the soul that sinneth, it shall die." And, like the children of Israel who felt death creeping upon them as the serpent's venom did its deadly work, so the sinner, young or old, when convinced of sin, is made to feel the "sentence of death" in his conscience. What is this sentence of death? It is a solemn knowledge of the fact, "By the deeds of the law, no flesh living shall be justified." One must come to feel this great truth, that "There is no one righteous; no, not one."

What must have been the pains of the children of Israel who were bitten, as they lay upon the ground writhing in their pain! The command was to "look and live," and yet multitudes lay there and died in the wilderness. Why? For one of the first effects of the serpent's bite is perversity in us, so that we do not wish to look; and they would not, they chose not, to gaze upon the serpent of brass. And boys and girls, before you can see beauty in Jesus that you wish to look upon, heavenly light to your eyes must be communicated. "The eyes of the blind must be opened." Many prayers go up from the hearts of godly parents and pastors that such a blessing might be bestowed upon you!

The serpent of brass was lifted upon a pole, and Jesus was lifted upon the cross; and by His obedient life and meritorious death. by His spotless righteousness and atoning blood, He brings life and healing to the sin-bitten. There are many boys and girls who now dwell in everlasting bliss who were led there because of these great truths. Godly Abijah is there, whose heart contained some good thing toward the Lord God of Israel; Samuel, who heard the call of God in early youth, and Timothy, who knew the Scriptures from his childhood, and thousands others were called by God's grace, in their youthful days – all who are now singing the song of the redeemed. O may the God of truth bless you, my dear young friends, and give you real conviction of sin, and put the Psalmist's plea within you: "O satisfy us early with Thy mercy; that we may rejoice, and be glad all our days."

Lessons From the Conies

"The conies are but a feeble folk,
yet make they their houses in
the rocks." – Proverbs 30:26

I can hear every reader ask, "What is a coney?" A coney is a little brown animal, something like a rabbit, which is found in the Bible lands. He is a little creature which inhabits the holes and the clefts in rocky places. I have been reading what natural history students have found out about the little conies, and I find some instructive lessons may be gathered from their habits and ways which will help me to set some moral truths before you. And I hope to shew you also how the conies preach the great truths of the gospel to us in a wonderful way.

May I shew you some good counsel and useful lessons which may be learned from the habits of the conies?

First, the wise little coney keeps on the beaten path round about his rocky dwelling. The conies go out in families to gather food, and they are very timid little creatures, so they keep to the paths which lead from their houses to where they obtain food to eat. The coney teaches a useful lesson, that *we must keep to the safe paths.*

What are the safe paths? They are the paths laid down in the counsels and admonitions of the Word of God – the paths of uprightness. I will now name some of these Safe Paths, for all boys and girls who read this, to tread.

There is the safe path of **Speaking the Truth.** O the unspeakable value of always speaking what is true! The foundation of a good character as a useful citizen is laid in speaking the truth. If you hear a man praised for his good character by those who know him, how do they usually

121

express it? You will always hear this: "I like Mr. Smith, for he can be trusted! He is a reliable man, and you know that what he says is truth." So, a boy or girl who possesses a character for speaking the truth is on the safe path.

"God is in heaven! Would He know
If I did tell a lie?
Yes, though I said it very low,
He'd hear it from the sky."

One day a little boy was bowling a stone along the road on his way home from school. The stone rebounded against the pavement and broke a window in a house. The owner of the house came out to see who had done such a deed and found the little boy looking at the broken pane. He said, "Did you throw the stone which broke my window?" The little boy replied, "Yes, I broke your window, sir; I was bowling a stone like you bowl a cricket ball, and it hit the kerb of the pavement, and rebounded through your window. I will try and pay for it." The gentleman was so pleased with his honesty and truthful answer that he said, "No, my boy, you shall pay only half. I will gladly pay the other half, because you have given me so much pleasure by telling the truth!" The path of truth is safe, children. Always speak the truth.

Another safe path is **Obedience to Parents.** "Honour thy father and thy mother," says God's commandment. The word of your father and mother is deserving of respect, and such respect should be shewn by carrying out the commands which they give you. Ask the poor man in the prison cell what was the first step he took in his downward road. In many, many cases, he will answer, "I was disobedient to my parents."

The Path of Honesty is also one of the safe paths. "Honesty is the best policy," an old saying goes. Let me tell you of a lad, who is now an aged minister of the gospel with an honoured name. As a youth he was employed by a corn-mill. One day, a man came to buy a quantity of corn, and the master sent the lad with the customer to fulfill his demand. As he was obtaining the corn, the customer said, "I will take two gallons instead of one." After he was gone, and the lad was returning to his master, a wicked thought sprang up: "You need not tell your master the man ordered two gallons; give him the money you were paid for the one gallon that he knows of, and keep the rest!" Alas, the lad succumbed to this evil thought. He put the extra money in his pocket and gave the other to his master. But a voice kept shouting in the lad's conscience: "Thief! Thief!" He could not rest, nor could he bring himself to spend the ill-gotten money. At length, he went and confessed his guilt and sin to his master, who forgave him, and from that day the master trusted him with many responsible tasks. From that day onward he enjoyed the esteem and love of many, as an honourable and useful servant of God.

Yet another safe path is **The Path of Kindness.** As the Lord Jesus taught us, to "do unto others as you would have them do unto you." Is there a more beautiful sight in all the world than seeing kind acts performed by boys and girls for one another? Do be kind to one another! In every way, avoid acts of cruelty and ill-temper; and help the afflicted in any way you can. I was touched one day to see a boy, on a very busy street in the city, go up to a blind man and lead him across the road and help him safely reach the pavement.

A lad, one snowy day, saw a poor, shivering girl in the street who was trying to sell holly to the passers-by. Her blue arms, as well as the basket on her back, were filled with great bundles of holly – so full her hands were not free to wipe the tears which were trickling down her cheeks.

"What's the matter, girl?" said the lad.

"My mother is ill and hungry," replied the girl, "and I did hope to sell my holly today, to get her some food. But nobody won't buy from me."

"Give me half of your lot, and see if I don't find some customers. You shall have some food," said the kind-hearted lad. And, taking a share of the prickly stock, he went crying out and calling before doors and windows, "Holly! Holly! Please buy some holly! For here's a little girl whose mother is ill and hungry. Who will buy her holly?" Not only was every branch of holly soon sold, but the little girl's basket was soon filled with all manner of odds and ends for her mother. Certainly you can see how that lad was treading the path of kindness! Boys and girls, an act of kindness – a word of sympathy – is never lost. The giver benefits as well as the receiver.

O may you tread the safe paths, like the little coney. Keep to the beaten paths of what is right. The Bible is filled with moral teachings, kindly warnings, wise counsels, and safe instructions, advice for every circumstance in the paths of life. It is the perfect guide-book for all who would travel in safe paths. "Wherewithal shall a young man cleanse his way? By taking heed thereto according to Thy Word." (Psalm 119:9).

I now want to shew you another lesson from the coney. *The coney is very cautious about food.* They will only eat the fresh, green provender, which they seek diligently. And I would affectionately warn you concerning poisonous food for the mind, such as bad books, novels, and erroneous literature, the conversation of ungodly companions and frivolous talk, and idle chatter.

The Word of God contains a striking story to tell us how necessary it is to be cautious about what one eats. Godly Elisha the prophet said to his servant, "Set on the great pot, and seethe pottage for the sons of the prophets. And one went out into the field to gather herbs, and found a wild vine, and gathered thereof wild gourds his lap full, and came and shred them into the pot of pottage; for they knew them not." But soon we read that, "it came to pass, as they were eating of the pottage, that they cried out, and said, 'O thou man of God, *there is death in the pot.'* And they could not eat thereof." (2 Kings 4:38-40)

Does not this sad event shew the wisdom and caution which is needful about the food we eat? Well, you say, my father and mother see to the food I eat, and so I am safe. Yes, and I speak by way of an illustration to thee: just as important as the food you eat is the books you read and the conversation you engage in! Can it not be said of many novels and writings that "there is death in the pot"?

The Lord wrought a miracle to remove the death in the pot at Elisha's dinner table. And when we read harmful books, or hear the suggestions of the ungodly, the God of truth must work a miracle for us to be healed of the diseases of mind it brings! Only the grace of God can counteract and conquer the harmful effects of poison which are imbibed in the mind from reading and listening to evil counsel.

Godly Mr. Tiptaft used to say, "Shew me a man's books, shew me a man's company, and I will tell you what sort of man he is."

Another habit of the coneys from which we may learn is, *The conies delight to gather together in companies and sit in the sunshine.* Does not this lead to another lesson? Does God cause them, by their nature, to do this, without instruction for us who are the image of God? What a pleasant sight to see children gathered at church, hearing the sound of truth. I love to see the boys and girls shewing attention in the chapel when the Word of God is preached, listening to its wonderful teachings. O, that you may feel what you sometimes sing:

"I thank the goodness and the grace
which on my birth have smiled,

And made me, in these latter days,
A favoured English child."

It is so good, to see boys and girls gathered together, to listen to good teaching – like conies in the sunshine – sitting in the rays of the Sun of Righteousness, as He shines the Word of God into their souls. Who can tell but what the eternal purposes of God may design some ray of light to communicate life to the dead! The promise runs, "My Word shall not return unto Me void."

I hope you will remember these lessons from the conies: 1st, The wisdom of sticking to the safe paths of moral principles. 2nd, The necessity of caution in eating the food which supplies the mind with knowledge. 3rd, The value of being found under the sound of the truth in church.

I also want to lay an important truth before you: the coney is "made wise" by a God-given skill. Yes, God has given the coney a natural instinct to hide from its foes and make its dwelling in the rocks. And the same God must make us wise by giving us heavenly wisdom to avoid the dangers and snares of life. *The Fear of the Lord* – a heaven-given principle. Yes, dear children, "The fear of the Lord is the beginning of wisdom" (Proverbs 9:10). Like the needle in the compass, which always points towards the north, so the fear of the Lord always points to what is right.

"By the fear of the Lord men depart from evil" (Proverbs 16:6). It is a straight, upright rule in the conscience which makes every wrong thought, word, and deed appear to be what they really are – wicked! O what a blessing is the fear of the Lord! The Word of God tells of a godly youth, in whose heart was found "some good thing" toward "the Lord God of Israel." This "good thing" in him was "the fear of the Lord"! And what a mercy if this good thing should be found within you. How it would rejoice the hearts of those who seek your eternal welfare.

O may this fact sink into your young hearts, and cause you to walk in safe paths and live upright lives! You must be made wise by the fear of the Lord. The blessed grace of godly fear, once implanted in your heart by the God of truth, will lead you to sing for joy.

But the greatest proof that the coney is "made wise" is how they preach the gospel to us in a wonderful way. The Word of God often refers to our God as a "Rock." Have you not joined in singing Toplady's beautiful hymn –

"Rock of Ages, cleft for me,
Let me hide myself in Thee."

"The conies are but a feeble folk, yet they make their houses in the rocks." O what a mercy if the Lord made you feel a need of such a wondrous Shelter! Have you ever thought about, why is the Lord Jesus likened to a Rock?

It is because a rock is a sure foundation, and Jesus Christ and His finished work is The Sure Foundation to every sinner. But only if the sinner starts to realize his condition as lost and guilty – like the tax-collector, who cried out "God be merciful to me, a sinner!" Only such a sinner feels the need of finding a sure foundation and wants to dwell in the Rock of Ages. No foundation, no shelter can be found beneath the sun which will provide protection from the storms of sin, a broken law, and hell and death. "Other foundation can no man lay than that which is laid, which is Jesus Christ."

O what a solemn fact that many, many set up a false shelter and build on a foundation which crumbles away. Yes, any religion which rests on a foundation of my own good works is "the works of the flesh" and is worthless in the sight of God. "All our righteousness is but as filthy rags." O, do not expect to get to heaven because you are "good" boys and girls, well-behaved. Such a foundation is "sand" and your house – your hope of heaven – will fall to pieces in the day of death, if resting on "good works."

It is a subject of eternal weight, a matter of awful importance: "What is my hope of heaven? Have I flown for refuge to Jesus Christ, the Rock of Ages?" The grave, death, judgment, and your eternal happiness or woe, are before you.

"O that boys and girls were wise,
Open, Lord, their closed eyes.
Bring with power this Scripture home,
Flee from wrath – the wrath to come."

The Word of God tells of a foolish man who built his house upon the sand. "And the rain descended, and the floods came, and the winds blew, and beat upon that house; and it fell: and great was the fall of it." (Matthew 7:27).

I went one bright summer day to see the ruins of a house which a foolish man tried to build on the sand. On the sunny South Coast, a huge pile of ruins can be seen not far from a famous watering-place. An ungodly man named Simpson vowed a vow that he would build a house on the sand, at the bottom of the chalky cliffs, where the waves roll every day, and he would live in it. He went to great expense, and huge loads of material were carried to the spot, and much pains spent to hold back the waves.

His house was built and finished, and looked a nice, substantial dwelling, but before the man could take up residence in his abode, the Word of God was soon fulfilled: "The floods came, and the winds blew, and beat upon that house; and it fell: and great was the fall of it." And today it stands a ruined heap, washed by the waves; and the folly of the builder and the truth of the Word of God is proclaimed by the name of that ruined heap – "Simpson's Folly" everyone calls it.

Boys and girls, "Except the Lord build the house they labour in vain that build it." The Lord Jesus Christ – His finished work – His doing and dying – is The Sure Foundation for you! All who go through heaven's gates are sinners who have been built as "living stones" on the Rock of Ages.

A rock is also a hiding place – a refuge. The coney's dwelling is his refuge and shelter, and the Rock of Ages, Jesus Christ, is a Safe Hiding Place and a never-failing Refuge to poor, needy sinners, who feel the tempest-tossing of the storms of life. O what a mercy, my dear young friends, to be safely housed in such an Hiding-Place! The sinner who enjoys such a blessing must be led into the Rock by the God of truth. A sinner must first be stripped, and made to know his undone state and ruin; and then he must be convinced of his just hell-deserving, and driven out of every "refuge of lies." Such teaching will bring him to want the good Toplady has written for us to sing:

"Naked, I come to Thee for dress,
And helpless, look to Thee for grace."

When a sinner is thus stripped, and brought down into the dust, he is being "made wise unto salvation," and he will feel and find in due time the Rock of Ages to be his Shelter and Foundation and Hiding-Place. His All-in-all, for time and eternity!

I have read that in the ancient city of Edinburgh, a "pound" was erected in the streets and a large letter "S" was painted on it. The letter "S" stood for *sanctuary.* A "pound" usually is an enclosure in a town into which straying cattle are placed until their owner is found. But this "pound" with the letter "S" upon it was for *men* – poor people liable to be thrust into prison for their debts. If a man was in debt and could not pay, the officer of the law would sometimes be sent to take that debtor to prison; but if the debtor were to escape from his house first and run into the "pound" for refuge, the officer of the law could not arrest him. Such a sanctuary was a safe hiding-place, and while he remained therein, his friends could seek means to help him to pay his debts, and then return home again.

The Lord Jesus is a Sanctuary of this sort to poor sinners, deep in debt to God through sin and wicked works. All sinners are debtors to the law of God, which has been broken by everyone who dwells on the earth. And if our grievous debt is not cancelled by Jesus Christ, the Law-keeper, we shall find God's broken law to be a millstone around our guilty necks to sink us down into everlasting misery.

The sinner who has been made to feel his guilt and debt, and who has fled for refuge to the Rock of Ages, is safe, and will dwell happily in a secure abode even when the world is in a blaze. As good Mr. Hart sings:

"They that in the Lord confide,
And shelter in His wounded side,
Shall see all dangers overpast,
Stand every storm, and live at last."

A Talk About Treasure

*"The kingdom of heaven is like unto
treasure hid in a field." – Matthew 13:44*

Many years ago, a peculiar people dwelt on the earth
called "alchemists." These men spent their days in seeking to
find out three things:

1st, A medicine to cure all diseases
2nd, A principle to turn base metals into gold
3rd, A powerful tonic to prolong life

These poor alchemists wasted away the precious days
of life attempting to solve the unsolvable problem of finding
a way for men to ever live and not die! But I have sometimes
thought of the fact that the problems which the alchemists
tried in vain to solve have a wonderful solution in the Word
of God.

The Word of God reveals, 1st, A Sovereign Remedy to
cure all diseases: "the precious blood of Jesus Christ, God's
Son, cleanseth us from all sin." The alchemist sought a "cure-
all" for *bodily* diseases, but the Word of God tells us of one
of God's names, Jehovah-Rophi ("I am the Lord who healeth
thee"), and a wonderful balm to heal the sin-sick soul
(Jeremiah 8:22).

And the Word of God sets forth, 2nd, A Marvelous
Power which works miracles in men and women, far more
wonderful than the turning of lead and ordinary metals into
gold. Who can estimate the wonders which have been
wrought by *the grace of God?* By this wonder-working
power, people with lion-like natures have been given lamb-
like dispositions, and many who have lived ungodly and
degraded lives have been changed into godly, upright, and

honourable citizens, and have left fragrant memories of a useful life.

And 3rd, A Real Cure-All for Life is revealed in the Word of God also! Jesus says, "But whosoever drinketh of the water that I shall give him shall never thirst; but the water that I shall give him shall be in him a well of water springing up into everlasting life."

The alchemists sought in vain to find out the knowledge which would unravel the secret of everlasting health and wealth, but this blessed secret is revealed to all who are brought to seek the Lord Jesus Christ from a felt sense of need. "Yea, if thou criest after knowledge, and liftest up thy voice for understanding; if thou seekest her as silver, and searchest for her as for hid treasures; then shalt thou understand the fear of the Lord, and find the knowledge of God." (Proverbs 2:3-5).

My dear young friends, I want to talk to you about Treasure – but something of a treasure far beyond the value of gold, silver, and precious stones. The Word of God is likened to a field containing treasure by Him who cannot lie. No tongue can tell the unspeakable value of the Word of God and an open heart to receive its blessed teaching. In Bible lands, men often hid treasure in the fields for safety in times of war and danger, and sometimes the owner would pass away without recovering his wealth, and so some farmer would later and unexpectedly find it.

What an amazing find that a *book* should contain treasure beyond price, and which will endure when the world is in a blaze! What makes the Bible such a valuable book? Look at the title: "*Holy* Bible." The word "holy" cannot be applied to any other book which ever came from a printing press. This book we call "Holy Bible" is The Word of God, and was inspired (which means, "breathed out" by God) from heaven. The God of truth voiced His mind from the realms of heaven, and enabled godly men to record His thoughts and words for man. "Holy men of old spake as they were moved by the Holy Ghost" (2 Peter 1:21). Never, never lose sight of this blessed fact, dear ones, that "All Scripture is given by inspiration of God" (2 Timothy 3:16). The Word of God is a "history" and a "mystery" book at the same time, and its records are true in every jot and tittle. We live in sad days, when ungodly men and so-called ministers criticize the Word of God, and assail its holy Authorship, but let all such critics and scoffers beware. The Word of God is called a *sword,* and all the enemies of truth will feel the keen, sharp edge when God deals with those who love a lie. O may the God of truth keep you who read these pages from joining the ranks of despisers of God's Word.

"O may we love the Bible!
God's holy book of truth!
The blessed staff of hoary age,
The guide of early youth;

The lamp that sheds a glorious light
On else a dreary road;
The Word that speaks a Saviour's love,
And shows the way to God."

I want to consider the word "treasure" in two ways:
1) Earthly Treasure
2) Heavenly Treasure

1st, Earthly Treasure. I want to prove to you ***the unsatisfying nature of all earthly treasure.*** The Word of God says, "Lay not up for yourselves treasures upon earth, where moth and rust doth corrupt, and where thieves break through and steal" (Matthew 6:19). Earthly treasure is affected by *the moth.* A man may be wealthy, and live in the midst of much earthly treasure. But time, like a moth, will surely and silently eat away his life, moment by moment, and every swing of the pendulum will bring nearer the day when he must depart and leave all earthly treasure behind. "We all do fade as a leaf." The longest-lived man on earth could not escape the ravages of the moth of time: "And all the days of Methuselah were nine hundred and sixty nine years; *and he died"* (Genesis 5:27). Yes, no matter how long this man lived, this man still died.

Earthly treasure is affected by *rust* also. What is meant by rust? Loss, disappointment, trouble, anxiety, pain and sorrow. "Man is born to trouble," and many who have abundance of earthly treasure have solemnly proved gold and silver cannot purchase case of mind and happiness. Rich clothing often bedecks a man and woman who has an aching head, a sad heart, and a dissatisfied spirit. Numbers of rich folk would gladly part with half their riches to enjoy the health given to many among the poor. A very wise man wrote in Ecclesiastes 6:1-2, "There is an evil which I have seen under the sun, and it is common among men: A man to whom God hath given riches, wealth, and honour, so that he wanteth nothing for his soul of all that he desireth, yet God giveth him not power to eat thereof, but a stranger eateth it: this is vanity, and it is an evil disease." And even when good health is enjoyed along with earthly treasure, still the rust will surely, in time, take it all away.

"No present health can life ensure
For yet an hour to come;
No medicine, though it oft may cure,
Can always pause the tomb."

And not only the *moth,* and *rust,* but *the thief* can take away earthly treasure. Many a wealthy man has found, to his terrible cost, that "thieves break through and steal." We may call Death a thief. The Word of God draws a solemn picture of a rich man who little thought of death coming like a thief in the night, in Luke 12:16-20. While the man was counting his treasure, and boasting of his accumulated goods, the thief was on the way to his dwelling. The message had gone forth: "Thou fool, this night thy soul shall be required of thee." Alas, my dear young friends, all earthly treasure stands in danger from rust, the moth, and the thief. Good Mr. Tiptaft often used to pray,

"Lord, make us truly wise,
To choose Thy people's lot;
And earthly things despise,
Which soon shall be forgot.
The greatest evil we can fear
Is to possess our portion here."

How much better to be found among the poor and afflicted family of God with the treasure of real religion than to sway a scepter over Britain's vast domain. "A little that a righteous man hath is better than the riches of many wicked" (Psalm 37:16).

I have read of a nobleman who was walking on his grounds with a godly man, and boasting of the extent of his possessions. "All these beautiful grounds, as far as your eye can reach, and these woods, they all belong to me," said he. "Well, my lord," replied his godly companion, "Do you see yonder little house? There dwells a poor woman who can say more than you, for she can say 'Christ is mine.' In a few years, all your possessions will be confined to the scanty limits of a tomb; but she will then have entered on an inheritance which is incorruptible, undefiled, and that fadeth not away, reserved in heaven for all who know the love the Lord Jesus Christ."

"Fading is the worldling's pleasure,
All its boasted pomp and show;
Solid joys and lasting treasure
None but God's own children know."

O may the God of truth give you an aching void which this world cannot fill, and enable you to esteem earthly treasure and this world's so-called "joys" as worthless things compared with a knowledge of Him, whom to know is life eternal. Then you will feel like the godly man who penned –

"Wealth and honor I disdain,
Earthly treasure - all is vain;
Nothing else can satisfy,
Give me Christ, or else I die."

But I have spoken to you of Earthly Treasure – now I want to speak to you of **Heavenly Treasure.** The God of truth communicates heavenly treasure to the hearts of poor sinners on the earth by giving them a felt conviction of sin and their sinnerhood. And many have received this wondrous blessing even in the days of youth. Conviction of sin brings a solemn sense of a sinner's state, which none can know or feel without God-given life. A man may go on pleased and satisfied with the things of this world, and heedless of what lies beyond the grave. Thoughts of the grave, death, and judgment to come are put into the background, and he feels no desire to be made ready to die. As soon as the heavenly treasure of conviction of sin is lodged in the heart, a man becomes the subject of new feelings. A great concern begins to bring him many anxious thoughts, and an aching void is felt which the pleasures of earth can no longer satisfy. And then, many questionings trouble the mind of such a man: "O what will become of me? I am a sinner; I must face the grave;

and what lies beyond for me – heaven or hell? Alas! I am a guilty sinner; I have broken God's law, and deserve eternal misery." Such a man can no longer go the way of the worldling; he is the subject of such feelings of misery and heart trouble that he cannot, dare not, stay any longer in the company of the ungodly. Conviction of sin leads to separation from the world, and brings a deep hunger and thirst into the heart which only the God of heaven can comfort and ease. The tax-collector felt this conviction of sin when he smote upon his breast and cried, "God be merciful to me, a sinner" (Luke 18:13). O what a mercy to feel one's self a sinner, and be found at the mercy-seat of Christ, waiting for the Lord to be gracious.

I have read of a case in which a happy young lady was blessed with the heavenly treasure of conviction of sin, merely by the word "eternity" being fastened on her conscience. She was living a butterfly life, going to parties and "the house of feasting," and was careless about things of eternal weight and importance. One evening she returned at a very late hour from some so-called pleasure, and going quietly into her room she found her godly maid reading by the fireside while awaiting her return. The maid did not hear the footsteps of her mistress, who, instead of attracting her attention, quietly looked over her shoulder to see what she was reading. The book was the Word of God, and her eye caught sight of one word and one word only: "Eternity". Such was the power of this word, the arrow of conviction pierced to the furthest depths of her conscience!

The maid, noticing her mistress, closed her Bible and attended to her duties, and both girls retired to their rest. In the night, the maid heard her mistress sobbing and lamenting, and being one who feared God, she went and enquired what the cause of her weeping was. The dear girl answered, amidst her tears, "O that tremendous word – 'eternity' – what shall I do? I am a sinner with a never-dying soul." O how glad the maid was to hear such things from the lips of her mistress, and to shew her the way of salvation by telling her "Jesus Christ came into the world to save sinners." The word of conviction proved to be a nail fastened in a sure place, and bore the hall-mark of heavenly treasure. She bade a lasting farewell to the ballroom and theatre, and was enabled to leave her gay companions, "Choosing rather to suffer affliction with the people of God, than to enjoy the pleasures of sin for a season."

Conviction of sin – that felt sense of our lost and ruined and helpless condition – is but a stepping-stone to the grandest blessing of all those which descend from heaven – the forgiveness of sins.

But conviction of sin, where it is genuine, will always be followed by the heavenly treasure of *repentance and confession of sin.* What is repentance?

> *"Repentance is to leave*
> *Those sins we loved before,*
> *And show that we in earnest grieve*
> *By doing them no more."*

No tongue can tell, no pen portray, the sighs and cries and groans of an awakened sinner. Sometimes the tear will steal down the cheek and, in the silent night, many searchings of heart will be experienced. The truth, like a searchlight, will be focused on the thoughts, words, and deeds, and the repenting sinner will conclude with Job, "Behold, I am vile!" And this knowledge will bring many strange-sounding confessions at the mercy-seat: "Unclean! Unclean! Woe is me!" O what a mercy to be the one who sees the grace of God and cries and sighs at Jesus' feet.

The spirit of prayer is also a heavenly treasure. A mere form of words is regarded as "praying" by many who think they will gain heaven by their good works, but real prayer comes from the heart.

138

"Prayer is the soul's sincerest desire,
Uttered or unexpressed;
The motion of a hidden fire
That trembles in the breast."

A minister was one day journeying on a country road when he heard a voice, and listening, he heard a man on the other side of the hedge praying, "God, be merciful to me, George Jackson, for I am a sinner." O what heavenly treasure in the heart such a cry reveals! Have you ever cried out so, boys and girls? A little while ago, I stood by the grave of a little fellow of eight years of age, who died as a rich possessor of heavenly treasure. He had been an afflicted lad, and he longed to be with Jesus Christ and sing the song of the redeemed. How encouraging to fathers and mothers, and to teachers of the Word, to know that little ones such as he are found there, singing Emmanuel's praise.

The treasure of *Faith* is yet another heavenly treasure that I would speak to you of. A man may read the Word of God through and through, and yet have no saving faith in Christ. "No man can say that Jesus is Lord" unless God gives faith to believe this wonderful truth. All saved sinners are blessed with a right knowledge of Jesus Christ as the Son of God. When Jesus dwelt on earth, men looked upon Him as a mere man; but if God gives us the heavenly treasure of faith, we shall say what Peter did: "Thou art the Christ, the Son of the living God." Many people only think of Jesus as a man whom the Word of God sets forth – "a good man," and nothing more. O what a mercy to have right thoughts of Jesus, and to feel Him to be "chiefest among ten thousand" to us. A heaven-sent faith will make a sinner cleave to Jesus with loving ties and esteem and admiration, and he will pine and long to know and love Jesus more, and mourn that he knows so little of His glorious Person.

This faith will make a sinner turn aside from the busy tumult of life to obtain a look, a word, a ray of hope from Jesus; and will bring many groans and longings and desires for grace to walk in the ways of truth. Godly men have joyfully laid down their lives because of their love for Jesus. What a marvelous strength the heavenly treasure of faith gives! One martyr, in the midst of the flames, shouted in joyous anticipation, "None but Christ! None but Christ!" O may the God of heaven enable my young readers to think upon this important question: "What think ye of Christ?"

This treasure of faith will prove a valuable help in times of trouble. Faith is sometimes termed "trusting in the Lord." A man may have an empty cupboard and empty pockets, and yet be "rich in faith." Who can estimate the volumes which might be written showing how the good hand of God has been opened to supply God's poor people with bread to eat! The cupboard shelves may be bare, and the last penny paid away; friends may fail, but the treasure of faith will enable a poor man to trade in a heavenly market, when the markets of earth are shut up. Say you, "Where is the market-place of heaven?" It is the Throne of Grace. And every blessed recipient of the treasure of faith can trade in this wondrous market-place.

A godly minister sat in the midst of his family one Christmas day, pondering the way in which the God of heaven had led him along through life. He had seen many ups and downs, and many, many times he had seen the goodness of God making crooked places straight. Up to that Christmas Day every need had been supplied, and he had found nothing fail of what God had promised. Many thoughts mingled in the mind of this godly man as he sat by the fireside, and as he reflected on past days, the pointed question came to mind, "Shall I not prove God's faithfulness also to-day?"

For lo, it was Christmas Day, and the dear minister's pocket was empty. No Christmas dinner seemed likely to appear to gladden the hearts of his little ones. Yet the minister would not give up the truth, "God is faithful."

When his wife began to complain and fret of it, he said to her, "I am sure, my dear, that the Lord will feed us."

The clock ticked steadily on and, bye and bye, it was too late to cook any dinner, and the grumblings of his wife were heard yet more: "No dinner for the children! What shall we do?"

"Put the cloth on, Betty," said the minister; "lay the table; who can tell? For the Lord's arm is not shortened. Let us remember the many helps we have received before."

"What is the use of laying the table, when there is no dinner to put on it?" moaned his grumbling Betty, as she spread the cloth and began to lay the knives and forks.

At length the hands of the clock pointed to the dinner-hour, and just about when the family would normally have been sitting down to their meal, a knock came at the door. O what a pleasant sight when that door was opened! There stood one who loved the godly minister for the truth he preached, holding a large tray containing a well-cooked dinner, all ready to be eaten! The good man had been impressed in heart with a sense of the minister's need, and had brought this dinner as a token of his love and esteem.

O how the sight of this dinner changed the faces of the waiting family! The minister joyfully voiced his gratitude as they all sat down, and then, turning to his shamefaced wife, he said, "Betty, the good hand of God has provided a dinner for us, but you had such a fearful heart, He would not allow you the pleasure of cooking it."

Yes, my dear young friends, the treasure of faith brings a blessed trust and reliance and confidence in God to help when all earthly streams are dried up.

But there is yet one brighter jewel, the brightest of all heavenly gems of treasure, found in the heart of those who know the grace of God.

It is the treasure of *The Forgiveness of Sins.* There is no truth more blessed than this: "Christ died for our sins."

Many who have been taught of God, and led to seek for mercy, have feared lest the blessing of forgiveness would never be enjoyed and felt. But the promise is sure: "If we confess our sins, He is faithful and just to forgive us our sins, and to cleanse us from all unrighteousness." Many have waited and waited many years and years to feel that their sins were forgiven, but for this blessing, "Blessed are all they that wait for Him!"

A young maiden of seventeen years of age went into Providence Chapel in the city of Cranbrook many years ago, when Rev. Isaac Beeman was preaching. The God of truth opened her eyes and caused her heart to receive the truth, and she was brought down in the dust of repentance to cry for mercy. Youthful days passed away, and grey hairs came, and still she was kept waiting and watching for the joy of the forgiveness of her sins. She passed her 90th birthday, still waiting and watching, and was nearly an hundred years of age when the God of truth enabled her to take down her harp and sing on the top-note of joy, "I know that *my* Redeemer liveth."

The things of earth which are termed "treasure" do not deserve the word. Gold and silver cannot make a dying pillow comfortable, or give comfort to a troubled heart. Health and wealth, good name and friends, have the word "passing" stamped indelibly upon them. I would rather live on bread and cheese, and break stones by the roadside for work, while enjoying "good hope through grace," than to be the butterfly of fashion and the popular idol, and dwell in the mansion of the rich. If I did not possess God's saving grace, I would have nothing! For how awful, to stand on the brink of eternity with only a good name in this world, or a little of its goods, and still be found numbered with the goats and shut out from the happiness of heaven.

I do pray that God, who searches men's hearts, will search yours, and bring you to seek "the Pearl of great price" – Jesus Christ – and may He be found in your hearts as the your sole hope of glory. For our days are numbered. The time is short, eternity is real and sure; and none can tell how soon our eyes will be closed to earthly scenes. What then? Will it be heaven or hell for you?

These heavenly treasures I have spoken to you of – are they found in you? Ask yourself: Do I experience heart-felt conviction of sin? Do sighs and cries and groans of prayer go up from my heart? Do I feel the tremendous weight of eternal things on my conscience? Do I feel Jesus Christ to be my chief desire, my Hope, my Refuge? Happy are the people who possess such things.

Never, never forget these facts, my dear young friends, and that the chief thing in this life is to be well-prepared to die. We are bound to an eternal destination – will it be heaven or hell? No line can fathom the depth of eternity. Count the blades of grass. Number the grains of sand; no arithmetic can number the years which count off "forever and ever."

Upon returning from a walk amid the falling leaves of autumn, Mr. Tiptaft once remarked, "I have been thinking of the tremendous fact that I must live in an eternal condition for as many years as the number of leaves on these trees, and the number of leaves which have ever grown upon these trees, and fallen off, too – and then, if I could count those, eternity will only have begun."

O may the God of truth drop His heavenly treasure in your hearts! What a mercy, if the prayer of Dr. Doddridge should be put in you:

"Engage this roving, sinful heart,
To fix on Christ, the better part;
To scorn the trifles of a day,
For joys which none can take away."

What the Earth Will Teach You

A Short Sermon From an Ancient Preacher

"Speak to the earth, and it shall teach thee." – Job 12:8

I want to tell you of a very, very old-fashioned preacher who has been preaching sermons, day and night, for thousands of years. This persistent preacher is The Earth upon which we live. Did you ever imagine that the Earth would speak to you? Yet it does, daily.

"What does the earth preach to us?" say you.

"Dust thou art, and unto dust shalt thou return" (Genesis 3:19) is his message. What a solemn fact this is! I am made from the ground that I tread beneath my feet. Our bodies are sometimes spoken of as "clay tabernacles." The Word of God tells us: "the Lord formed man of the dust of the ground" (Genesis 2:7). The minister who stands by the open grave at a funeral service says: "Earth to earth; ashes to ashes; and dust to dust."

Death is the solemn theme of the sermons preached by the Earth, and every tombstone and green mound over the dead echoes, "Amen." O may the God of truth give my dear young readers ears to hear this preacher's voice! The grass which waves in the breeze today, and is cut down by the scythe tomorrow, proclaims this message: "All flesh is grass." The flowers which fade and the falling leaves remind us: "We all do fade as a leaf." And you have seen the trees marked with the white cross, awaiting the woodman's axe.

145

"Like crowded forest trees we stand
And some are marked to fall;
The axe will smite at God's command,
And soon shall smite us all."

I have read of a king in olden days, who gave a feast to a number of his friends, and when they were gathered at the meal-table, he bade them look up. Over every man's head hung a sword suspended by a thread. And truly, our life is like a brittle thread, and who can tell how soon the thread may break?

Jesus said to His friends, "But one thing is needful; and Mary has chosen that good part, which shall not be taken away from her" (Luke 10:42). O how it would rejoice the hearts of those who seek your eternal welfare to find you anxious to possess that "good part!" That "good part" is to know and love the Lord Jesus Christ, and to be always sitting down at His feet to learn the truth. The Lord gave Solomon wisdom to choose "the good part" and O, may He give this same heavenly wisdom to you.

Yes, boys and girls, "The fashion of this world passeth away," and all that is under the sun is soon to be gone. Only those who know Christ will last!

A young man who was highly acclaimed for his knowledge of mathematics lived in a village where a godly minister was stationed. One day the minister met the young man, and, after some conversation, when they were about to part, the minister offered him a parting thought.

"I have heard that you are renowned for your mathematical skill; I have a problem which I wish for you to solve."

"What is it?" enquired the young man.

The minister replied, "What shall it profit a man, if he shall gain the whole world, and lose his own soul?"

The young man at first scoffed at the question as unworthy of his thought, like it were a silly riddle. He returned home, endeavoring in his mind to shake off the minister's problem, but it was in vain. Again and again the question rose back up in his conscience, and he soon was brought to feel that the one thing needful was to be following Jesus Christ.

O what a pleasant sight when those who are still youths join with Moses in "choosing rather to suffer affliction with the people of God than to enjoy the pleasures of sin for a season."

A godly minister, who taught in a Sunday School, once had a very naughty scholar of a lad in his class, named Joseph, who tested his teachers' patience often by his mischievous deeds. He was so full of evils that they knew not what to do with him. But the God of heaven looked down upon this boy in mercy and opened his eyes to see his condition as a guilty sinner before God, and laid him in the dust at Jesus' feet, and here is how it came to pass. One day, he was playing out of doors with a number of ungodly companions, and he stopped to carve his name in the bark of a tree. Suddenly he heard something pass his ear like a gust of wind, and it was as if the words came to his conscience, "I will bring thee to judgment." He felt the stings of a guilty conscience, and left that place bowed down with great conviction of sin, and feeling, "I shall be in hell before I get out of these woods." It proved to be the beginning of a good work of grace in him, and he spent many days lamenting his sins and crying out for mercy.

He came to his minister, a Mr. Taylor, saying "I am a lost sinner!" Mr. Taylor replied, "Joseph, you have had much good instruction in the Sunday School, have you not?"

"But I hated it then," he said, "and now I remember everything. All my sins are before me now. God is just in condemning me. O what will become of me?"

The good work was continued, and soon poor Joseph was brought to know that Jesus had died even to save *him,* and he rejoiced with unspeakable joy.

Such cases as this provide encouragement for godly fathers and mothers, teachers and ministers, to continue to sow the seed of God's truth among the young. For he that goeth forth and weepeth, bearing precious seed, shall doubtless come again with rejoicing, bringing his sheaves with him. For God will make "good ground" in the hearts of many, ready to receive the seed of grace, who find the Word of God to be a word of life eternal. May you be among them!